Feb 1987

Tina Gogo

Also by Judie Angell
IN SUMMERTIME IT'S TUFFY
RONNIE AND ROSEY

Judie Angell
Tina Gogo

BRADBURY PRESS   SCARSDALE, NEW YORK

Special thanks to Arthur Kornhaber, M.D.—J.A.

1 2 3 4 5   82 81 80 79 78
The text of this book is set in 12 pt. Electra.

Library of Congress Cataloging in Publication Data
Angell, Judie. Tina Gogo.
Summary: Living in a small resort town where her family runs a restaurant, eleven-year-old Sarajane meets and befriends an unusual girl with a mysterious past.
[1. Friendship—Fiction. 2. Restaurants, lunchrooms, etc.—Fiction. 3. Foster home care—Fiction] I. Title.
PZ7.A5824Ti   [Fic]   77-16439
ISBN 0-87888-132-8

For the Music Man

Tina Gogo

Chapter One

"Sarajane? Sara! *Sarajane!*"

I could hear her. I was only around the side of the house, but Mama had a shriek that could've brought a mole clear out of the ground.

"*Sarajane!*"

I gritted my teeth and stayed where I was. It was getting toward lunch time, and Mama wanted to be back at the restaurant to help Pa serve the lunch crowd. Big crowd. Three truckers and Wilma from the beauty parlor.

That left me to take care of the Pests.

"Saraj-"

"I'm coming!" I'm coming, darn it.

"Didn't you hear me calling you?" Mama said when I got to the back stoop. "I called and called! Didn't you hear?"

"Only the last one," I said.

Mama smiled. "Well, I've got to go. The kids are upstairs. What's that on your toenails?"

"Nail polish." I said. "Frosted Rose Petal."

"It certainly is. Say, how would you like to take the kids to the movies this afternoon?"

"Oh, *yeah!* I would! Can we go with you to the restaurant and eat there first?"

"Sure," Mama said. "I'll fix you sandwiches. Don't you want to know what's playing?"

"Oh. Yeah. What's playing?"

"I dunno," she said and went back into the house, yelling for my brother and sister. Bo is seven and Katie is nine. I'm eleven, which means I'm responsible for them. I was also responsible for them when I was nine and they were five and seven, so I can't see why Katie can't be responsible now that *she's* nine.

They came down the stairs when Ma yelled "Movies." I didn't blame them. Summer vacation was only a week old but it felt like a hundred degrees in the shade. Our house wasn't air-conditioned, but the movie was. So was the restaurant, but it was no fun hanging around there, because if you're there, you have to work.

I stepped into the kitchen and slammed the screen door behind me, but two flies got in anyway.

Bo bounced in. "Sarajane, we're going to the movies!" he cried happily. "What's that on your toenails?"

"Frosted Rose Petal."

"Y'got it all over your toes!"

"The grass smeared it," I told him. "Did Ma tell you we were going to have lunch at the restaurant before the movies?"

"Sure, that's why I'm wearing shoes. Aren't you going to wear any?"

"No. Where's Kate?"

"Here," she said. She had changed out of her overalls into a dress. One of my old pinafores. She got all my old stuff but she didn't seem to mind. Most of it came from Cousin Suzanne in the first place.

Our restaurant was the nicest one for miles. It wasn't like a luncheonette or anything, it was a real restaurant, with tablecloths and carpeting and drapes. But everybody in town kind of treated it like a luncheonette for two reasons. One, the real luncheonette burned down a year ago and nobody built it up, and two, Ma and Pa made cheap lunches for people because they really weren't very busy except in the tourist season, which was starting now. We had a big lake, called Lake Meridian, and it had motels and little cabins on it that people could rent, and nice sailing and terrific fishing. So a lot of people came to our town in the summer—some for a month or two weeks or a long weekend or even for the whole season. The restaurant did good business and it really carried us through for the whole rest of the year.

It was called *Punchy's*. Our name is Punch.

"You gotta choice of tuna, cold chicken or ham 'n' cheese," Pa said when we came in.

"I wanna menu," I said.

"You just had one."

"Tuna," I said.

"Chicken," Bo said.

"Ham. Hold the cheese," from Katie.

"You would," Ma said, putting on an apron and heading for the kitchen.

Pa was beginning to dress like he did for tourist season, with a pretty short-sleeved shirt and a tie. He never wore a tie any other time of year, except when there was a special dinner, like for the Rotary or the the Elks.

"What's the picture we're going to see?" I asked him.

"I think it's a Walt Disney," he answered. "*Bambi*, I think." He was putting silverware and cloth napkins on the tables.

"You think new people'll be coming in today, Pa?" Katie asked. Katie liked the restaurant, she was really at home there. She helped out almost every day after school, even though there wasn't much for her to do.

"You never can tell when it'll start," Pa said. "Hot weather hits, *Punchy's* is ready."

"Fourth of July we'll have a mob," Katie said. "We always do."

"Can I have firecrackers, Pa?" Bo wanted to know. He always asked that question, every year since he was four.

Pa always said the same thing. "Nope. You can watch the firemen's show down at the lake but don't you ever let me catch you with crackers or I'll take the skin off your rear!"

"Awwww. . ."

Meridian was the name of the lake, the town, and the movie theater. It was also the name of the junior high and high school, one of the motels, a gas station, a bar and the bowling alley. The elementary school where we went was just called the Cromwell Avenue School. Only I was finished with Cromwell. In the fall I would go to Meridian Junior High.

I thought about that while we walked over to the theater. Junior high. There had been some talk that there were too few kids to keep it going, and they were thinking of just keeping us on at the elementary school until it was time for high school. Well, it wasn't going to happen this year, I knew that much. I was looking forward to the new building. Seven years in one school is enough—kindergarten, plus six grades. Of course, the same kids would be there, but the school would make it seem new.

"Hey, it's not *Bambi*," Bo yelled. "It's *Cinderella*!"

"Goody!" Katie cried.

"Yuck, I don't wanna see *Cinderella*," he whined.

"Okay, Bo, just go on back to the restaurant and wait there all afternoon while Katie and I go," I said.

"Did you get candy money?" he asked.

"Yup."

"Then I'll go."

Bo sat still for the first ten minutes of *Cinderella* and then started wiggling and fidgeting. Katie gave him her candy money to keep him still but he finished off a box of Milk Duds in two seconds and was at it again.

"Hey, get your elbow off my armrest," Bo said to Katie. "Shh!" Katie said.

"Shh, wha?" Bo said. "There's only three other people in here!"

"Eight," I told him. "There are eight people. And it doesn't matter how many people are here. You're supposed to be quiet and let them enjoy the movie."

"I wanna walk around," Bo whined.

"Oh, let him walk around, Sarajane," Katie said. "I can't hear anything with him here."

"All *right*!" I hissed at him. "But don't you dare walk out of the theater, you hear me?"

"Yeah!" He leaped over my crossed legs and was up the aisle in two seconds. Two minutes later he was back, running down the aisle being chased by another little boy about his size.

"Bo!" I said too loudly, but he paid no attention

and ran across the stage, making shadows on the screen, followed by the other boy.

When I got up out of my seat to chase Bo, I saw another girl running down the opposite aisle. She was after the other kid and she caught him before I got to Bo.

"Georgie, I'm gonna kill you," the girl said, and she grabbed his hair and smacked the side of his face with her palm. He put up both his hands and sank to the floor at the girl's feet.

Bo had stopped at the side of the stage and was just watching. So was I. I was afraid of that girl. I never hit Bo or Katie in my life. I never even thought about hitting them, even when they were acting up, like Bo just was. Anyway, I probably would've caught it myself if I hit either one of them.

The boy made a face at the girl and she gave him another smack on his shoulder and dragged him back to their seats, which happened to be right next to where I was standing.

She looked up at me and frowned. "What're *you* starin' at?" she asked.

"Nothing," I said, staring at her.

"Quit it," she said. "Go get your kid. And tell him to leave Georgie alone, or it'll be him that gets it next time."

"Your brother was chasing *him*," I said, getting a little mad.

"He's not my brother and watch your own mouth," she said. I looked down at them. There was another little boy with them and when I squinted my eyse, I saw he looked exactly like Georgie. Twins. The girl

Bo was still at the side of the stage but he had sat down on the steps and was just waiting, I guess, to see what I was going to do. I walked over to him, took his hand, and led him back up the aisle to our seats. When we walked past the girl and the twins, Georgie stuck out his tongue at us.

"Who are they?" Bo asked. "They don't live here."

"Maybe they're summer people," I said. "They must be."

"She really hurt him, did you see?" Bo said.

I didn't answer. Katie missed the whole thing, watching Cinderella get dressed for the ball.

We sat back in our seats and just as I was getting involved in the movie, I saw the girl coming up the aisle toward me. I suddenly felt scared.

"Hey," she whispered.

"What?"

"You got any money?"

I stared at her.

"There you go again, starin' at me. Don't you understand English?" she said.

"Leave me alone," I said nervously.

She twisted her mouth and shook her head. "I'm not gonna hurt you, dummy. I just wanna know if you have any money for candy or something. Popcorn. We could share it. How old are you?"

"Eleven."

"I am, too. And I've got two kids to watch and *you've* got two kids to watch, so we might as well sit together and watch all four of them."

"I don't have any money," I told her. "Bo already ate up all our candy money."

"Oh," she said, and started toward her seat.

But a few minutes later, back she came again, dragging the twins behind her by their sleeves. They slid into the seats directly behind us.

"What's your name?" I heard directly in my ear. I jumped and turned around so quickly I banged my nose into the side of her cheek.

"Jeez, I didn't mean to scare you," she said. "I just said, 'What's your name?' "

"Sarajane," I mumbled.

"Did you say 'Sara' or 'Jane'?"

"Both," Bo said, turning around.

"Two names?" she asked.

"Yeah, sort of," I said.

"What's your last name?" was the next question.

I wanted to tell her she sure was nosy, but I didn't.

"Punch."

"What?"

"My last name's Punch."

"You're kidding," she said and started to giggle. I could feel my face get hot and red.

"She's not kidding," Bo said angrily. He was braver than I was.

"Punch!" said the twins and started to laugh. The

girl smacked them both on the head with one hand, whipping it back and forth. "Shut up!" she said.

She leaned forward again. "Listen," she said. "I'll tell you my name. It's not so hot, either."

I didn't want to know her name but I didn't tell her that.

"It's Bettina."

"So?"

"Bettina Gogolavsky."

Now it was my turn to giggle. Bettina Gogo— what?

"Okay, we both laughed at each other's names," she said. "Now we can sit together. You sure you don't have any money? Why don't you check your pockets?"

"I don't have any. What was your name again?"

"Gogolavsky. But you know what they call me?"

"What?" Bo piped up. Bettina glared at him and turned back to me.

"Tina Gogo."

"Two nicknames," I said.

"Yeah. This movie stinks," she said.

Katie finally had had it, got up and moved over several seats.

"What's the matter with *her*?" Tina sneered.

"She likes the movie. She wants to hear it. Are you summer people?" I asked.

"What's 'summer people'? "

"Are you here for summer vacation? I mean, I live here all the time, and I've never seen you before. Or them." I nodded toward the twins.

"They just moved here. George and Teddy Samios. They're twins."

"I can see that. What about you?"

"I'm here for the summer, I guess," she said.

"You guess?"

"Yeah. Have to see if I like it."

Georgie leaned toward Bo. "How old are you?" he asked.

"Seven," Bo told him.

"We are, too. What's your name?"

"Bo."

"I'm Georgie, he's Teddy."

Bo said, "You look the same to me."

"I know," Georgie said, "but you can tell us apart. Teddy don't talk much."

The movie was practically over. The only one who wanted to see the end was Katie. The other two people in the theater were making out the whole time, so they didn't care if we were talking. I was pretty sure it was Linda Merkel and Earl Peterson. They were seniors in high school. It was kind of hard to tell, they were so close together.

Chapter Two

We walked outside together when the movie was over, and just stood under the marquee. Tina didn't look like she was in a rush to get home and I sure didn't want her coming home with me, so we all just kept standing there.

"Are you babysitting for them?" I asked Tina, nodding at the twins.

She frowned. "No. They're my friends." She tilted her head. "Why?"

"Oh, no reason. I was just wondering if you were getting paid for watching them."

"Nah. What's the matter with your toes?"

I could feel my face get hot. Why did I put that dumb nail polish on anyway? "The grass smeared my nail polish," I said almost in a whisper.

Katie was getting impatient. "C'mon, Sarajane, we gotta get home."

"Uh, yeah," I said, and turned away. "See ya," I said over my shoulder.

"Hey!" Tina called. Here it comes, I thought. She's gonna ask if she can come.

"What?"

"Where do you live, anyway?" she asked.

Bo, who had been hanging back with the twins, answered right away. "Howland Road," he said. "You know where the Fire House is?"

Tina shook her head.

"I know," Georgie said and pointed. "Up that way."

"Yeah, well it's the first left turn after the Fire House. You just keep on going and we're the last house on the right. The end of the street. It's a dead-end street, that's why we have this big yard . . ."

"Come on, Bo!" Katie said. He skipped toward us.

"Maybe we'll visit you," Georgie called, and they all just stayed there watching us go.

"I thought they were going to come with us," Katie mumbled.

"Me, too," I said, as Bo ran on ahead. "What a funny kid."

"Funny?"

'Not funny ha-ha," I told her, "funny peculiar. I mean, she's not *friendly*, but . . . she doesn't exactly leave you alone, either."

"Yeah," Katie said. "For sure!"

I looked up in time to stop myself from bumping into Rosemarie Rice, my friend from school. She was loaded down with shopping bags and nearly didn't see me either.

"Hi, Rosemarie! What's all that?" I asked her.

"Hi, Sarajane. Hi, Katie. This is stuff for my summer job," she said. "I've got to get it all together by next weekend so I can start working right away. I need a lot of new school clothes this year."

"What's your job gonna be?" Katie asked.

"Oh, I'm teaching macrame classes to the summer people. Kids and grownups. I've been practicing all winter and spring and I can make lots of nice things!"

"Hey, that's a good idea," I told her. "Wish I could take a class with you . . ."

She laughed. "Well, you can in the fall—after the tourists go home. Then you won't be so busy."

"Maybe I will. See ya, Rosemarie."

"See ya, Sarajane. 'Bye, Katie!" and she disappeared into Peckman's Drug Store.

"Boy, it's really *next* weekend!" Katie said, smiling to herself. "Are you excited, Sarajane?" She meant the Fourth of July. It was Meridian's biggest weekend of the whole year, because it was the real official beginning of the tourist season. Just like the Labor Day weekend was the official end. For us, the Fourth of

July always starts on a Thursday. Instant Busy, Mama says. Thursday night, the motels and cabins are filled. The ones that haven't been booked ahead of time are filled by last-minute people. The restaurant is jam-packed every night and even for lunch, and Wilma has to brown-bag it to the beauty parlor until September.

"Well, are you?" Katie asked. "Excited?"

"Guess so. Except it's a lot of work," I told her.

"But that's fun!" she said with a big grin.

"It's fun when you're nine," I answered. "It's work when you're eleven."

Ma was back from the restaurant when we got home and was waiting for us. Bo was already outside, playing under the sprinkler.

"How was the movie?"

"Oh, good!" Katie said.

"That's nice," Ma smiled. "Listen, Sarajane, you know those menus we had printed last month? I can't remember where we put them."

"You mean the ones with the new prices?"

"Yes, where are they?"

"The ones with the list of 'Things to Do in Meridian' on the back?"

Mom folded her arms. "Yes . . ."

"The ones with the picture of the lake on the cover?"

"Sarajane, if you don't . . ."

"Haven't seen 'em."

"SARAJ-"

"They're in the basement! In a box! Near the furnace!" I jumped away, laughing as she grabbed for me.

"Well, go and get 'em, you little stinker," she said, swatting me on the behind. "I want you to draw some of those little flowers on the back. You know the ones you do that look like lilies of the valley swirling around?"

"Oh! Yeah," I said. Gee, Mom thought my drawings were good enough to put on *Punchy's* menu! "You want me to make them like a frame around the list on the back? Like a border?"

"Sure, that'd be pretty," Mom said. "I'd appreciate it, honey."

I spent the rest of the afternoon drawing on the menus and I even took the ones I hadn't finished down to the restaurant to work on during and after supper. Ma and Pa liked them a lot.

The next day was Thursday. We all got up early because it hadn't been very busy the night before. There were a few new people but not too many and us kids hadn't had to go home before Ma and Pa. Ma was on the phone when I came down for breakfast.

"Well, I know you'll be packed full by a week from today, Martha, but what can we expect for the beginning of the week? . . . By tonight? You sure? . . . Well, how about Jessie and Ralph? . . . all coming next Thursday, huh? What about the Land's End? . . . Right, I'll check with them. Thanks, Martha." She hung up and turned to me. "Sarajane, Martha's

.16.

got two families checking in tonight, but as far as she knows, most everyone'll be coming up Thursday over the Fourth. I'm going to be on the phone for a while checking on the other places, but I want you to take a pile of those menus you were working on last night, go down to the lake, and get them tacked up near the front desks in all the offices."

"Is it okay if I eat first?" I asked.

Ma laughed. "I'm sorry, honey. *I* ate and I completely forgot that my kids didn't! Go call Bo, he's outside." She hollered up the stairs for Katie.

I opened the screen door and stepped outside. Bo was playing catch. With the twins.

"Hi."

I looked down. Tina was sitting below the stoop on the cellar door. "Took you long enough to start moving around," she said.

"How long have you been sitting here?"

"Since about seven," she answered. It was eight-thirty then.

"Well . . . what do you want?" I asked her.

"*I* don't want anything," she said. "The twins wanted to play with your brother, so I brought them over. That's all. I see you took that stuff off your toenails."

"Hey, listen, I've got some chores to do. . ."

"Some what?"

"I've got stuff to do. I have to work." I told her. "Bo doesn't have to go. Ma'll be here so they can stay and play. But I have to eat and then go."

Tina shrugged. "I don't care," she said. "I'll stay till you finish eating."

I yelled for Bo and he and the twins came running. I started to say, "Not you," but Ma opened the door just then and Bo and I had to introduce everybody.

"Well, breakfast is ready . . ." Ma said. "Did you kids have yours? . . ."

"No!" Georgie cried. Tina and Teddy just stared at Ma.

Ma sighed. "All right. Come in." The twins tripped over each other rushing through the door.

"*Katie!*" Ma called. "Get down here! I'm not working short order in my own house!"

Katie appeared immediately, took a look at Tina and the twins and shrank back. She went over to the counter with her plate and began to eat standing up.

"You here for the summer, Tina?" Ma asked, dishing out pancakes.

"If I like it," Tina said, her mouth full. It was what she had said yesterday at the movies.

"What do you mean, 'if you like it'?" I asked.

"What words don't you understand?" she said. "I mean if I like it I'll stay and if I don't I'll leave. Period."

"Isn't it up to your parents?" I asked. What was she so mad about?

"I'm not here with my parents," she answered and played with the syrup bottle. "I'm staying with this . . . family. Just for the summer. While my mother is traveling."

"Traveling where?" I asked.

Tina glared at me. "None of your business," she said. I looked over at Ma, but she was busy cleaning up the stove and I guess she didn't hear. "In Europe, if you must know," Tina said, not looking at me. "She's just seeing the sights. You know, the Leaning Tower of Pisa and the Eye-ful Tower, stuff like that."

The three boys finished eating and began to head for the door. Without looking up from the stove, Mama called, *"Bo?"* And Bo came back, picked up his plate and brought it to the sink. He left the twins' plates.

"Who are you staying with?" I asked Tina.

"I told you. This family."

"Well, yeah, but who? I mean, we know just about everybody in town," I said.

"You don't know them," she said. "They don't live here. They just rented one of those cabins for the summer. They're from Queens, New York."

"I know *Queens*," I said. She talked like I was from the boonies or something. "New York isn't *that* far from here. Lots of the summer people commute to New York City every day. Some of the townies do, too."

"Well, it sure seems far to me," Tina said. "Can I have more milk?"

Ma turned around. I could tell from the look on her face she was going to say something about "please" but for some reason she didn't and poured

Tina another glass of milk. Then she sat down in Bo's chair next to me.

"Now look, Sarajane," she began, "when you bring those menus around, you stay there and make sure whoever's in charge tacks them up right away. Don't let them say they'll do it later, that's when they get lost. And you make sure it's in a good place when it's put up, not behind a bunch of notices. Okay?"

"Yeah, well, you can't miss 'em," I said. "I mean, look at the size of them. They're twice as big as last year's."

"Well, for good reason," Ma said, heading for the cellar stairs. I brought my dishes over to the sink. Katie was still at the counter and she hadn't said a word. "Would you do these for me, Katie?" I asked. "I have to get the menus out."

She nodded. Tina stood up, leaving her plate on the table. "What menus?" she asked. "What was she talking about?"

"Mama and Pa own a restaurant," I explained. "It's called *Punchy's* because of our name. And the food is good. You can tell your . . . family about it. What's *their* name, anyway?"

"Harris," Tina answered. "I call them Jim and Emily."

I picked up Tina's plate and the twins' and took them over to Katie who had already begun to wash the dishes. "What's the matter with you?" I whispered to her. Katie was quiet, but she usually had *something* to say.

"Nothing."

"Well, I'm going now," I told her. "With the menus. Tell Ma I'll be back in plenty of time for her to get down to the restaurant for lunch. Okay?" Katie just nodded again. "Are you okay?" I asked.

"Jeez, yes, Sarajane, would you just go?" she said. I shook my head at her and went to the door, followed by Tina.

"How come you have so much to do?" Tina said as the screen slammed shut behind her.

"How come you don't?" I asked.

"My mother says I never have to work if I don't want to," she answered, kicking a stone.

"Really?"

"Oh, yeah. I can just do whatever I want. We don't need any money, we're rich."

"I never heard of anybody that didn't need any money," I said. "How come your mother didn't take you to Europe with her? Didn't you want to go?"

"Naah," Tina said. "She says I'd be better off here in the country." She turned to me. "That's stuff's boring, you know? Going on one plane or another all the time. Suitcases . . . who needs that?"

"Are the Harrises friends of your mother's?" I asked.

"You sure are nosy, y'know that?" she said, picking up her kicking stone and throwing it.

"Where's your father?" I asked.

"Helping the President run the country," she answered.

My eyes opened wide. "Really?"

"Shut up," she said.

"I never knew anybody as angry as you," I said, shifting the pile of menus to my other arm.

"I never knew anybody as nosy as *you*," she said. "Listen, my father died, okay? Now do you feel better?"

"Listen, I don't care if your father died!" I yelled. Oh, my God. "Hey, I didn't mean I don't *care* if your father died." I stopped walking. "What I mean is, you don't have to be *ashamed* or anything. I mean, you don't have to get so mad at me. It's not your fault your father died." I felt just awful.

"I'm not ashamed," she said. "Who said I was ashamed?"

"Okay, okay. Look, I have to go in here."

We had arrived at the Meridian Motel, the biggest on the lake. Martha Beck ran it with her husband, Frank. She was in the office behind the desk when we came in.

" 'Morning, Sarajane. Who's your friend?" she said cheerfully.

" 'Morning, Mrs. Beck. That's Tina."

"Hello, Tina."

Nothing from Tina.

"I brought our new menu," I said. "Ma said could you put it up now?"

"Sure, honey," Mrs. Beck said. "You pick out the best place for it on the board." She pointed toward the bulletin board opposite the front door. The only things on it were a notice about a party for the high school teachers which had taken place two weeks ago, and an announcement of the firemen's fireworks show for the Fourth of July. I put a bright red tack through the inside page of the menu and smacked it right in the middle of the board. I heard the door slam behind me as Tina walked out.

"Thanks, Mrs. Beck," I called as I began to leave.

"Oh, wait a minute, Sarajane," she said looking up. "You put that down too low. It should be eye-level."

I looked at the menu. "It *is* eye-level," I told her.

"Not *child's* eye-level, honey," she said, smiling. "Put it higher, so it'll be grown-ups' eye-level. They're the ones with the eatin'-out money!"

"Thank you," I said, and moved it up.

Outside, Tina was kicking a stone against a tree.

"What'd you slam out for?" I asked, beginning to walk to the next stop. She followed behind me, slowly, but didn't answer me, so I just kept walking. After a minute, she caught up. I kept looking straight ahead.

"Any minute *she* was probably gonna ask me questions, too," she said, almost whispering.

I started to say, "Even if she did, so what?" but I didn't say it. What I did say was, "Everybody always asks questions when a new person comes into town. They don't mean anything by it, they just want to get to know you better is all."

Tina said, "I don't want anybody to get to know me better."

"Even me?" I asked, and looked right at her.

For the first time, she smiled. Well, it wasn't really a smile, but her face did something or other that I hadn't seen before. She said, "Ahhh, you're okay, S.J."

S.J., I thought. Boy.

The next stop was the Karefree Kabins. There were four little cabins with kitchen privileges. The people who rented them usually cooked their own food, but if they ever got bored with that, like Pa says, *'Punchy's is ready.'*

I looked at Tina to see if she was coming in with me, but she just shook her head and stopped at the end of the path, kicking a circle in the dirt with her toe.

Jessie Hart was in charge of Karefree. She always told me to call her "Jessie" intstead of Mrs. Hart. She said it made her feel younger. I figured she was probably around fifty, so if she wanted to feel younger she was entitled to.

"Hi, Jessie, can I put up a menu?" I asked. She was folding sheets on a cot in her little office.

"Sure, Sarajane. Where do you want it?"

"Where's the best place?" I asked.

"Over at the Meridian," she said and cackled.

"I've been there. How about taping it to your desk, right in front?" I suggested.

"You'll be a good businesswoman, child," she said. "That'll be fine."

"How many cabins you rent so far?" I asked, taping the menu to the edge of the desk.

She sighed. "Only one. Oh, but guess who it is, Sarajane?"

"Mr. Hopper!" I cried.

"Right!" she said happily. "Isn't that nice? All you kids enjoy his stories so much! 'Member last summer how you all sat up on the porch of Kozy and just listened and listened?"

"Oh, he was good . . . He'd take all the different parts and he had different voices and everything . . ."

Jessie clapped her hands together. "Oh, I remember," she smiled. "I used to sneak up behind the railing and sit and listen myself."

"Well, 'bye, Jessie. Thanks for the space." I nodded at the menu.

Tina was still making circles in the dirt when I came out.

"All excited over a bunch of kids' stories," she sneered.

"Cut it out . . ." I said.

". . . And if you're good, maybe you all get a cookie afterward!"

"Stop it!" I said. "These stories are different. Besides, if you're not going to come in, you shouldn't listen at doors!"

"Are you kidding?" she said. "You could hear an ant sneeze through a screen door like that, for Pete's sake. Who's this guy, Hopper, anyway?"

"I dunno, he's just a guy," I said. "I think he's a writer. Once he said he was testing out his material on us kids. He lives in the city, that's all I know. Come on." We had arrived at Land's End, one of the smaller motels. The Harmon family ran it and they had so many kids, there was always someone around working.

"Wanna come in this time?" I asked her. She shook her head. I bit my lip and thought for a minute. "Hey, Tina?"

"What?"

"Y'know, Meridian is really a nice vacation town. Especially in the summer. You could have a good time. I have a lot of things I've got to do, like mind the kids at mealtimes while Mama and Pa work, and clean up at home and things like that. And if you want, you can help me, or we can do things afterward or something . . ."

She didn't say anything, so I went into Land's End and left my menu. When I came out, she was there, standing with her hands behind her back like she was waiting to be called on in school.

"You going to the Shoreline?" she asked.

"Is that where you're staying? The Shoreline?"

"Yeah. But they're cook-in cabins, too."

"I know, but I gotta leave a menu anyway," I said. "Where do Teddy and Georgie live?"

"The Shoreline. Their parents bought it."

"No kidding! I didn't even know it was for sale."

"Thought you knew everything in this hick burg," she said.

I made a face at her.

"Anyway, it wasn't for sale, exactly, it was kept in the family. Mr. Samios's sister owned it with her husband and they just sold it to him. About two months ago."

"They told you that?" I asked.

"They told the Harrises," she said. "I just overheard."

Gee, I thought, I wonder if Ma knows about the change of owners.

The rest of the places we reached through the woods. We could have gone back up to the road but it would have been silly to. I knew the shortcuts. All we had to watch for was poison ivy.

"There any other kids in this town?" Tina asked me. "I mean, like our age?"

"Sure," I said. "But we all work in the summer. Some of the girls are mothers' helpers, they take care of little kids while the parents fish or swim or sail or something. And some of them work at our place . . . They're mostly older, though. Some kids teach sailing, on the little Sunfishes. I don't know, everybody works. You could probably get a job if you wanted . . ."

"I don't want a job," she said. "I don't even know if I'm staying here, for Pete's sake."

"Well, where would you go, then?" I asked her. "If you left, I mean."

She picked a leaf off a tree. "I dunno. I could always get on a plane and meet my mother somewhere. Or I could go back to the city and stay with my father . . ."

I whirled around. "Your *father*! You said—"

"I don't mean my father," she said, quickly. "I mean my uncle. He's really my uncle, but he lives with us and I . . . think of him like a father. I mean, he's the

.27.

only man I've known. Around the house, I mean."

"How come he didn't go to Europe with your mother?"

Tina gave me a look that I'd seen before. It always went with her "You're too nosy" hollerings. But she didn't say that. She just said, "He has to stay home. He owns a big department store."

"Oh." I looked at my watch. "It's a quarter to twelve!"

"So?" Tina said. "It's a quarter to twelve. So what?"

"I have to get home, so my mother can go to work." I hadn't finished delivering all the menus, but I did get most of them. I could do the rest when Ma got home after lunch.

"How about if I come with ya?" Tina asked. "I could eat lunch over."

I looked at her. I never knew anybody that asked things like that. You're supposed to wait to be invited. But boy, I thought, I'd seen a whole lot of Tina the last two days and she hadn't been invited yet!

"Well . . ." I said and sighed. "All right. Go and ask and I'll meet you home." I turned away.

"Go and ask who what?" she said.

"*You* know. The people you're staying with. Don't you have to ask if you can go out for lunch?"

"The Harrises? Why should I ask them anything? I can do whatever I like. Let's go."

I just stood there.

"*Well?*" she said. "Are you coming or not?"

"Yeah," I said. "I'm coming."

.28.

Chapter Three

The sound of Canadian geese honking their heads off as they flew over the lake: that's what I woke up to the next morning. The summer people think that sound is real pretty, but *I* think I'd rather wake up to soft music or something.

I rolled over and tried to go back to sleep, but I couldn't. It would be busy at the restaurant starting now, I thought. Nothing like the Fourth, but a lot busier than, say, February.

I got dressed and went downstairs to the kitchen, where Katie was hanging over the stove.

"Sarajane, this year Mama says I can cook!" she bubbled.

"You can't cook anything, Katie," I said. "What can you make?"

"Omelets!" she said, smiling. "I've been learning to make cheese omelets. Pa's been teaching me, sometimes in the afternoon, sometimes at night. I'm real good at it. Want one?"

"No thanks. I just want cereal," I said. "That's good, Katie, that you can cook. What are you going to do, hang around the restaurant and wait for somebody to order a cheese omelet?"

"Yup!" she said.

I smiled at her. It was okay with me, then I'd only have to watch Bo. But it didn't seem like any way to spend a summer.

Ma came into the kitchen. "Sarajane, have you met Mr. and Mrs. Samios yet?" she asked.

"No," I said. "Why?"

"Just wondering." She began to do the breakfast dishes neither Katie nor I had done. "I never really knew their relatives, you know, the people that owned the place before. They weren't involved much in town things, since they didn't have any kids."

"Well, they're going to be living here all year round, Georgie says, so I guess we'll get to know them."

"Dry these, Sarajane," Ma said, tossing me a towel. "I'd better go down and introduce myself pretty soon. Be a nice thing to do, and besides it's good business."

"They're cook-in cabins, Ma," I reminded her.

"Makes no difference," she said.

The kitchen door opened and slammed closed.

"Hi, Tina," Ma and I both said together without turning around.

"It ain't Tina, it's just us," Georgie said. "Where's Bo?"

"Where's Tina?" I asked, surprised. I hadn't seen the twins yet without her.

"Guess she's sick," Georgie said. "She didn't come out of her cabin this morning. Where's Bo?"

"Upstairs."

Georgie started up the back stairs, but Teddy just stood there, watching the stove.

"Breakfast is over, Teddy," I told him. "The kitchen is closed." He started up after his brother.

"Hm!" Ma said. "Wonder what's wrong with Tina?"

"I don't know, but I guess we'll have a morning of peace and quiet for a change. What am I supposed to do today?" I asked.

"Glad you asked," Ma said. "Keep an eye on Bo, of course, but I'm going to have to get down to the restaurant a lot earlier today, which means the burden of the housecleaning's going to fall on you . . ."

"What about Katie?" I asked. "Before, she always helped."

"Well, she wants to learn to cook, honey, and she has a knack for it. I'd like her to learn, she could be a real big help down there."

I just frowned and looked at the floor. Mom lifted my chin with her hand.

"You know, if Katie gets good, and she really likes it, *she'll* be the one helping Pa in the off-months and I'll get to spend more time at home here."

That made me smile and I felt better. Why the heck would *anybody* want to spend their time *cooking*?

What I had to do was: dust all the window sills and lampshades and lightbulbs; take a broom to the ceilings to get rid of the cobwebs; wipe all the knicknacks on the shadowboxes; try to get the mold off the upstairs shower; and change and wash the bedding in Bo's room because sometimes he still wet the bed. Doc Redditch said it was because his bladder never woke up his brain when it was time to go, so he just kept on sleeping. Or something like that.

During the morning, Bo played outside with the twins and I did my work inside. I sang songs to myself and had kind of a nice time, even though a cobweb did fall off the broom and land in my hair.

At lunch time I was going to send Georgie and Teddy home, but figured what the heck and made them all pancakes. It was easy, with the mix. All you do is add water. They burned a little, but those kids didn't care.

"Don't you have to call your mother?" I asked Georgie. "Won't she expect you home for lunch?"

"Nah. We told her we'd be eating here," he said, stuffing his mouth.

My mouth dropped open and I stared at him.

"GEOR-gie . . ."

"Wha?"

"How'd you know you'd be in-vited here—for—lunch?"

He chewed a while, then swallowed noisily. "Well, we *were*, weren't we?" he said and I felt like I'd asked a really dumb question.

I decided to drop it. "Listen, you guys want to go swimming this afternoon? Shall I take you down to the lake? A lot of new kids'll be down there and it would be a nice way to meet them."

They mumbled excitedly and shook their forks. I think their mouths were stuck together from pancake syrup.

At about one-thirty I figured we could go. Everything was finished. I had even hung out Bo's sheets on the line. The kids were working on Bo's rabbit trap in the back yard. It wasn't the kind that would hurt a rabbit, just catch one. It had a kind of cage door that dropped down when the rabbit went into the cage after the bait, a carrot. Pa asked what if a skunk went in there instead of a rabbit but Bo said no way could that happen. Anyhow, Pa suggested that Bo build himself a doghouse along with the rabbit trap so he could sleep in it in case the rabbit turned out to have a white stripe down its back.

I got them inside to get out of their clothes. Bo only had one bathing suit but most of the time, he and the other kids swam in their cut-offs. So the twins just had to take off their shirts. Then I put on my own bathing suit.

"We'll leave our stuff here," Georgie said, "and come back after we swim."

I threw his shirt over his face. "Sorry, Georgie, we're not adopting you. Sometime you're gonna have to go home. Your mother will forget what you look like."

I grabbed four towels and started down the back stairs, just as the kitchen door creaked open and slammed shut.

"MA?" I yelled and walked a little faster.

Tina was standing there.

"How come you never knock?" Bo asked.

Tina ignored him. "You going down to the lake?" she asked me.

"Well, yeah. What are you doing here? I thought you were sick."

She stepped back a little and put her hands on her hips. "Do I look sick?" she said.

"Jeez, how do I know!"

"Don't go to the lake," Tina said. "Stay here. The kids can go under the sprinkler."

"I don' wanna go under the sprinkler," Bo whined. "I wanna go to the lake!"

"Tina," I said quietly, "I promised the kids we'd go to the lake. You can come if you want, or not."

Tina stepped in front of the door. "Come on, S.J. . . . If I go down to the lake . . . I'm gonna get caught . . ."

"By who? For what?"

"Oh, I happened to mention to the old lady that I didn't feel good this morning . . ."

"What old lady?" I asked.

"Harris," Tina said, like I should know. "Anyway, that's all she hadda hear, she made me stay . . ."

"Is she an old lady?" I asked.

"Will you let me finish, for Pete's sake?" Tina yelled. "No, she's not so old, that's what you call people, that's all. Just a way you talk. Anyway, I had to stay in bed with nothing to do and after a while I felt better. So when she went out to get groceries I split and came here."

"She's going to be mad at you," Bo sang at her.

"So what!" Tina snapped. "She'll find out I'm around sooner or later."

I wondered whatever happened to my peace and quiet. "Hey, Tina, I'm goin' to the lake," I said, and moved toward the door.

"Okay," she said. "You wanna go? We'll go."

I shook my head at her and we all walked out of the house together, the three boys skipping ahead. "Don't go in the water till I get there, Bo," I screamed at him, but he didn't answer.

When we got down to the dock, all three were in the water. I made Bo get right out and sit on the grass for five minutes as a punishment for disobeying. He kept crying "I didn't *hear* you, I didn't *hear* you." But it didn't make any difference—it was always the rule that he couldn't go in the water unless someone was watching him. So he knew.

Tina was looking nervously around.

"Why don't you just go home instead of waiting to be caught?" I asked her.

Suddenly she grabbed my arm with icy fingers. "Look" she said, nodding at the top of the hill where you enter the swimming area.

"At what?" I wanted to know.

"Don't you see that cop?" Tina whispered.

"Are the police after you?" I said, scared.

Tina took a deep breath. "That one is," she said. "It's old man Harris. He's a New York City cop. Ain't *that* a kick in the head!" she said and laughed.

"He's not so old . . ." I said, squinting at him.

"You dummy, I told you that's just the way you talk. Dammit. He must've gotten off work early and now he's comin' lookin' for me."

"Well, go meet him," I said. "Don't wait for him to come down here and be mad at you."

"Maybe he won't see me," she said.

"He'll see you," I told her. "You're the only one wearing a sweater in 90-degree heat."

Sure enough, the policeman seemed to spot us and came walking heavily down the hill.

"A cop," Tina mumbled. "Wouldn't you know I'd have to be living with a cop. Boy, would they laugh, back in the city. Tina Gogo, a cop's daughter!"

"What do you mean, 'daughter'?" I asked.

"What I mean is," she said very slowly, "that I'm

living with this guy for temporarily while my mother is traveling and so for that time, while she is away, I am like their child. Do you understand that?"

"I guess . . ."

"That's all I meant."

Mr. Harris came toward us and stopped. Tina looked him square in the eye, the whole while, with her chin sticking out. He looked back at her and nobody talked.

Finally, Mr. Harris said, "Do you have any idea how worried Emily's been about you?" He said it very quietly.

"Well, she shouldn't be," Tina said, still staring at him. "I was just around. I never went far."

"You were sick," Mr. Harris said.

"Well, I'm not sick now," she sneered. "So bug off!" She never looked away from him.

I could see she was really pale and shaking a little. I guess Mr. Harris could see it too, because he didn't say anything about how fresh she was. He just waved his arm toward the top of the hill.

"Let's go," he said.

Tina stood there. "What are you gonna do," she said, "arrest me?"

Still he didn't get mad. Just jerked his head toward the Shoreline Cabins. "Get up there," he said to her. "Go on. Show Emily you're all right. Then we'll talk."

This time she went, but she was glaring at him until she finally had to turn around to see where she was going.

Then Mr. Harris turned toward me. "Are you Tina's friend?" he asked.

"I guess so," I told him.

"Tina been spending her time with you the last few days?"

I nodded.

"What's your name?"

"Sarajane," I answered. "Sarajane Punch. My mama and pa own *Punchy's*. The restaurant up on Main Street?" Mama trained me always to mention it to summer people whenever I could work it into the conversation without sounding pushy.

"Oh, yes," he said. "Looks nice from the outside. We'll have to try it sometime."

"Yessir," I said.

"Sarajane, wonder if you'd do a favor for us," he said.

"Yessir?"

"Maybe you could . . . When Tina comes over to see you, maybe you could ask her if she told us where she was going. We, uh, we worry about her, you know, when she doesn't . . . I mean, I know she's okay, but I'd like to know just where she is, and so would my wife. You think you could do that?"

"Sure," I said, nodding. "I could do that."

"Thanks," he said smiling at me. Then he turned and went up the hill.

That night we all went to the restaurant, Bo and me included. This was the beginning of a lot of weekends of hard work for Mama and Pa. My job was to set up the tables and also wash and dry dishes because there were a lot of extra ones used. Bo just dried and separated silverware. Katie did some fried stuff and was learning to decorate desserts.

"Sarajane," Mama called from the kitchen, "show Earl how to fold those napkins right, will you?"

Earl Peterson came out of the kitchen then, with a waiter's red jacket on.

"Hi, Earl. I didn't know you were working here," I said.

"Hi, there, Sarajane. Yeah, your pa hired me this morning. I was supposed to work over at the gas station, but Travis came home last night so his father gave him my job."

"I thought Travis was going to Arizona to work on a ranch this summer," I said. Travis Sumner was a year older than Earl and went away to State College. His father owned the Meridian Gas Station.

I began folding napkins like teepees and Earl copied me.

"Well, that job fell through," he was saying. "They'll be sorry, though. I'm a better mechanic than Travis is, any day."

Earl's napkin looked like a doughnut instead of a teepee.

"No, look, you tuck it in *here*," I said, showing him. "You as good a waiter as your are a mechanic?" I asked him.

"I better be," he said, "or I'll lose this job, too. It

was nice of your pa to hire me at such short notice. Only thing is . . ."

"What?"

"Takes up most of the night, you know? Won't be seeing so much of Linda. How's this?"

His napkin looked more like a teepee, but the side was dented.

"Stand it up like this," I said. "That's better. Now do another one." I handed him the flat cloth that still smelled from the laundry's iron. I love that smell and feel of cloth. When I was younger I used to wind it around and between my fingers and hold it up to my face so I could get that clean smell. I wrecked a lot of clean napkins and got a lot of clean smacks.

"Sarajane!" from the kitchen. I left Earl folding and stepped through the swinging door.

"Ma?"

"Here!" she tossed a dishtowel at me. "Go 'round to all the tables and make sure no glasses have spots. Then see that all the water pitchers have lots of ice in them, and that there's one for each station." She was cutting tiny lemon sections to put beside the tomato juice glasses. "Then come on back in here and have your own supper so you'll be ready when we need you. Okay, honey? Hurry up, now."

The waiters were supposed to check on the clean glasses before they put them out, but they didn't always do it. Sure enough, I found four glasses with spots.

While I was having supper in the kitchen, Earl came in with an order and said, "Sarajane, there's a kid out there asking for you. Table, uh, five."

"Asking for me?"

"Yup. Hey, Miz Punch, did I write this down okay?"

Ma looked at Earl's pad. "Sure, Earl. Three steaks, all medium rare, one baked, two mashed, salad, no soup. Just fine, Earl."

I got up and skipped out quick through the swinging door so I wouldn't get in anyone's way. Tina was at table five with Mr. Harris, who wasn't wearing his uniform, and I guess, Mrs. Harris. I walked over to the table.

"Hi," I said.

"Hey, S.J." Tina said.

"Emily, this is Tina's friend," Mr. Harris said. "Sarajane Punch."

Mrs. Harris smiled at me and nodded.

"You eatin' in there?" Tina asked, nodding toward the kitchen.

"Sure," I told her.

"I wanna eat in there with her," Tina said, getting up.

"No, Tina," Mr. Harris said. "Tonight we're eating as a family. Together, here. You said you'd like to eat in a restaurant and that's why we're here. Now sit down."

"I wanted to come here so I could eat with *her*,"

Tina said, pointing at me. I began to get nervous. Other people were coming in and Tina was getting loud.

"Tina, please . . ." Mrs. Harris said softly.

But Tina was on her feet.

"Tina, you can't eat in the kitchen," I told her. "Nobody's allowed in there but the help. That's the rule. Sit down. You're gonna have a good dinner." I started to back toward the swinging door, a bad mistake. You have to look where you're going if you're going to work a restaurant. "See you later," I said, turning around and crashing into Earl, who let fly a tray full of tall glasses of tomato juice, saucers, and tiny lemon sections.

Ma was there in a second and between her, Earl, Scotty—another waiter—and myself, we got it cleaned up pretty fast. But Earl's jacket was wet and he wasn't too happy, even though I kept telling how it was all my fault.

"Anyway," I said to him, "it doesn't show. It's tomato juice, same color as the jacket."

"I need this job, Sarajane," he muttered angrily at me.

"I'm sorry, Earl, everybody knows it wasn't your fault. I'll stay out of the way. Promise." And I went back into the kitchen to get yelled at by Ma and Pa. I didn't go out again, and I didn't see Tina the rest of the night, but when we were cleaning up later, Earl apologized again to Ma and Pa. Ma said she knew he wasn't to blame for the fortieth time.

"Who was your friend, anyway, Sarajane?" Earl asked me.

"Oh, that was Tina. She's here for the summer. Why?"

"The whole summer? I didn't think she was gonna last through dinner," he said.

"What do you mean?"

"Didn't you hear her clear into the kitchen? Man, she was yelling at her poor folks like crazy. They were really embarrassed. They didn't even stay for dessert, even though they paid for it. I mean, they didn't order *à la carte*."

"I heard her," Ma said. "What was she so mad about?"

"Everything," Earl said. "Right, Scotty?" Scotty Helfin worked as a waiter for us all year round. He went to Northport Community College, which wasn't far, and he paid his way with what he made from Pa. Plus he tutored four high school kids in math.

"Was that the one who threw her napkin at the guy?" Scotty asked.

"Yeah. I don't know what was bugging her. Guess she wanted to be in the kitchen with Sarajane. She really ticked me off. You hear her laugh when Sarajane crashed into me?"

I hadn't heard that. I was too busy being upset.

"I was worried she'd make the customers nervous," Mama said, scraping crumbs from one of the tables into a pan. "Good thing it was in the early evening. They were gone by the time the real crowd came in."

"You picked a winner, Sarajane," Earl said.

"I didn't pick anything," I told him.

At nine o'clock Mama told me to take the kids home. The rush had long since slowed down and there weren't too many people left in the dining room. Those that were there were finishing up. Pa said they were New Yorkers. New Yorkers never ate dinner before nine or ten o'clock, he said. I wondered how anybody could wait that long.

Bo and Katie went right to bed, but I stayed up and waited until the folks got home. They looked beat.

"Sarajane, it's eleven-thirty!" Ma cried when she saw me. "You're not even in your pajamas!"

"I wanted to wait for you," I said.

"It's okay, Flo, I'm glad she's up," Pa said. "I want her to hear my idea."

"Oh, your idea!" Mom snorted. "I'm telling you, I think it's too much."

"What's too much?" I asked.

"Your pa wants to open for breakfast this season," Ma said. "He only wants to spend his waking life working!"

"The town really needs it, Flo," Pa said. "Since the luncheonette burned down, where are the folks going to get something to eat that time of day? We could really do well!"

"We're doing well," Ma said, flopping down on the sofa. "And we need our rest. Besides, folks can always get coffee and rolls at the drug store."

"They can get better ones at *Punchy's*," Pa insisted. "And eggs, too. Katie's learned to make good omelets."

I looked from one to the other as they talked. I didn't want them to work in the morning. They'd never be home. And that meant there'd be extra housework for *me*.

"Look, we could alternate in the mornings," Pa was saying. "We both don't need to be there. I'll have Earl, and Scotty, too, if we need him. And between one of us and Katie, it'd be smooth as silk. Come on, Flo . . . We'd have it made!"

Ma said, "Let me think about it."

"You can't think about it too long," Pa said. "We have to do it right away, if we're going to. So's we can get established, and people know they can count on us. If we wait too long, they'll have found other places. Over in Northport or something."

"What do you think, Sarajane?" Ma asked, knowing what I thought. I bit my lip and looked at the floor.

"The kids need us at home, Mike," she said.

"The kids'll have one of us at home every day. We need the money, Flo," he said softly. "The kids are getting older and things are getting more expensive, I don't need to tell you . . ."

Ma shook her head. "You're going to do it anyway. Doesn't matter what I say . . ."

"It does matter," Pa said.

"Then don't do it," Ma said firmly.

"I have to do it, Flo," Pa said. And to my surprise

Ma burst out laughing. Then Pa started laughing, too.

"What's so funny?" I wanted to know.

"The way we always arrive at big decisions around here," Ma said. "Come on, honey, let's go upstairs."

She took my hand, something she hardly ever does any more, and we went into my room. She took my pajamas and robe out of the closet while I took off my cut-offs and shirt.

"You could've insisted," I muttered at her. "You could have said you wouldn't do it."

"Yep, I could've," she said, putting my clothes in the laundry bag.

"Hey, not the cut-offs," I cried. "I want to wear them tomorrow!"

"Sarajane, these shorts are going to stand up by themselves if you wear them one more day." She sat down on the bed next to me. "Look, honey, I could have told your Pa that I just refuse to work mornings. And you know what he would have done? He would have said, okay, Flo, that's fine, don't worry about it, and he would have gone down there every morning by himself. Or I could have gone even further and said I didn't want *him* to do it, either . . ."

"But?" I asked.

"But you know, the first time he got a look at the price of shoes in the fall, he would have done a double flip."

"Awww . . ."

"And besides, it's only for the summer. Remember that, Sarajane. There's a long winter coming."

Ma kissed me and tucked me in. I still like it when she does that, and it doesn't make me feel like a baby. Well, maybe it does, but I still like it. I fell asleep thinking that maybe there was a long winter ahead but it sure was hard to imagine it then . . .

Chapter Four

The Fourth of July fell on a Sunday. Pa said the weekend people would probably stay for the fireworks show and either leave late that night for the city, or wherever they came from, or go home late Monday afternoon. Dinner at *Punchy's* was served early the night of the show, so Ma and Pa could close early and see it. Pa said it was the best fireworks show on the east coast. I don't think he ever saw one to compare it to, but I sure liked it a lot anyway.

The volunteer firemen were in charge of it and what they did every year was, they built a big 1776 out of wood, mounted it on a raft, and floated it out into the middle of the lake. Then, at the end, after the crackers and rockets had gone off, they set fire to the 1776 so the whole thing was in flames and they set off more skyrockets all around it. It was gorgeous. We never got tired of seeing it.

Katie and Bo and I usually had a quick supper at the restaurant and then took our blanket down to the lake about seven-thirty, even though they never started before nine. We spread our blankets out on the grass to reserve our places and then we could go play or even swim if it was hot.

Some of the Harmon kids, whose family ran the Land's End Motel, usually had a concession where they sold cold sandwiches and soda, popcorn and candy and stuff like that. One year, Charley Harmon got into a fight with Neddy Sumner because Neddy opened a lemonade stand right near the Harmon concession. Charley's pa worked it out by telling Neddy he could have his stand but it should be moved to another part of the area, so from then on Neddy was a regular, too. He even managed to rent a helium tank and sold balloons for fifty cents a piece. Pa said that was pretty good for a thirteen-year-old kid.

Both Neddy and the Harmons were all set up and ready for business when the kids and I got there, which was earlier than practically anybody. Except the Samios twins, who never seemed to be with their parents, just each other. They came and grabbed Bo just as soon as they saw him.

"You stay where I can see you," I warned him. "Don't you go off and get in any trouble."

"I won't," he whined. "We're just gonna play catch till the show starts."

"Okay, but you know where the blankets are. You get back here in plenty of time," I called after him as he ran.

Katie and I sat down on our blanket. I had brought my Frosted Rose Petal nail polish and this time I was going to do my toenails right. No running in the grass so it could get smeared. I'd paint 'em real nice and just lie quiet until they were dry. Wilma's feet looked so nice in sandals when her toenails were painted.

I took out the bottle and began to brush each nail carefully.

"You doin' that again to your feet?" came a voice above me.

I didn't even look up. "It's pretty if it doesn't smear," I said.

"It's dumb," Tina said and sat down.

"I'm going to help sell at the Harmon's stand," Katie said and took off.

"How come your sister runs away every time I come over?" Tina asked.

"I dunno. Does she?"

"Yeah, she does," Tina answered. "What do I need, Listerine or something?"

"How do I know? Where's your family?" I asked.

Tina sneered. "You mean the cop and his wife?

They're not here yet. How long do we have to sit around before they start the action?"

"They never start before it gets dark," I said. "But nobody's forcing you to stay. You can come back when it starts." I finished doing my nails and closed the bottle.

Tina didn't say anything, just stayed where she was. Suddenly she reached for the nail polish bottle.

"What do you think you're doing?" I asked.

"What does it look like?"

"Looks like you're painting your nails. Thought you said it was dumb."

"It *is* dumb," she said. "Doesn't mean I can't do it." She painted all her toenails and when she was finished with them, she started drawing red circles around her knees with the polish.

"Hey!" I yelled. "Don't do that. You're wasting it!"

She yanked the bottle out of my reach and, holding it up high, finished the circles.

"*That's* dumb," I told her. "Circles on your knees!"

Tina just laughed and blew on the circles to dry them. "The circles go with these stupid shorts, don't you think?" She had on a pair of pink shorts with little daisies on them. Finally, she handed me the bottle and I put it back in my overalls pocket.

"Where are the twins and Bo?" I asked Tina. I looked around and couldn't see them at all. The beach wasn't that big.

"Saw them a minute ago," she said. "They're somewhere."

I got up. "Yeah, but where? I gotta keep an eye on Bo. Especially at the water."

"They'll be back, S.J. Sit down," Tina said and lay back on the blanket.

"No, I'm gonna look. You stay here in case he comes back." I went to the Harmon kids' stand first. "Katie, have you seen Bo?" I asked her. She and Betty Harmon were already busy, selling popcorn to all the kids who arrived before their parents.

"We sure did," Betty Harmon said, as she made change for a little boy. "He was with two nasty little brats who tried to steal a bag of peanuts from us."

"*Bo* did?" I cried.

"No, not Bo," Betty said. "One of those twins he was with. I caught him, though. Darn near broke his arm. Those rich city kids think they can get away with anything!"

"They're not city kids," I said. "At least not any more. They live here. Their parents bought the Shoreline."

"Oh, no!" Betty groaned. "They'll be here all year round? Lock up your silverware!"

"Is that Bo up there?" Katie asked, pointing to the hill. "No, I guess not. Looked like him for a minute . . ."

"Where could he be?" I asked. "I told him not to get out of my sight."

Katie said, "Well, somebody distracted you . . ."

Just then there was an explosion. Everybody jumped and looked around. There's a kind of an echo to sounds when you're around water and it's hard to tell where the noise is really coming from.

People began to run and Katie and I followed. They were heading toward the Karefree Kabins. I ran into Ma and Pa halfway up the hill. They were just arriving.

Ma caught me by the shoulders. "Sarajane, what *is* it? What's going on?"

I started to cry. "I don't know . . . Did you hear that big noise? I can't find Bo . . ."

"Oh, my God!" Pa said, and turned and hurried after the crowd.

Ma took my hand and followed him. "What do you mean, you can't find Bo?" she asked very quietly.

"He went to play with the twins. I told him to stay in sight, but . . ."

"But then Tina came and Sarajane was talking to *her*," Katie said.

"Just for a minute . . ." I started to say, but we had reached the cabins. There was a crowd around Kozy Kabin, the one Mr. Hopper always rented. I felt a little sick. Pa broke out of the crowd when he saw us coming.

"It's okay, it's okay. There was an accident, but everyone's all right . . ." he was saying to Ma, who couldn't say anything.

"Bo?" I cried, pulling on Pa's shirt. He looked down at me. "Sarajane, we trusted you to watch him. How could you let him go off the beach area?"

I was really crying by this time. "I don't know, I

don't! I'll never do it again, honest! Please . . . what happened . . ."

"Just a minute," Pa said. He left us and went back into the crowd. A second later he was back, with Jessie Hart, who was holding Bo. Bo was crying, too.

"You tell your mother what you did," Pa said to Bo. I could tell he was furious, because his voice always got real quiet when he was angriest.

Bo was sobbing. "Nothin', I didn't do nothin'! It was Georgie's idea, and it was Georgie who did it!" He clung to Jessie and cried harder.

"Tell her!" Pa said.

Bo stopped crying instantly. "Well, Georgie thought it would be fun to, uh—borrow—some firecrackers and set them off ourselves. He said he used them in New York, he said he knew how, he said . . ."

"And what did you do when he said that?" Pa asked.

"Nothin'! *He* did it!"

"Did you say, 'No, Georgie, that's dangerous, and I'm not allowed to play with firecrackers'? Did you?" Pa said.

"Well, I didn't take 'em . . ." Bo said, snuffling.

"Did anyone get hurt or not!" Ma practically screamed.

"Thank God, no," Jessie said. "They were all just scared silly, but at least they were smart enough to get well out of the way before the thing went off."

Pa and I saw the twins at the same time. They were being dragged away from the crowd by a man and a lady. The lady had one twin and the man had the other, each by the wrist. Teddy was crying. At least I think it was Teddy—I just couldn't picture Georgie crying.

"Just a minute!" Pa said as they passed us. Teddy stopped crying and they all looked at us. "Mr. and Mrs. — uh —"

"Samios," I said.

"Mr. and Mrs. Samios?" Pa asked.

"Yes?" the man said.

"I'm Mike Punch, Bo's father. I want to talk to you about what your boys did . . ." Pa's fists were clenched.

"They're gonna get it, believe me!" Mr. Samios said, glaring at Georgie.

Mrs. Samios had tears in her eyes. "Isn't there someone who is . . . to guard these things . . . The firecrackers . . . ?"

Jessie spoke up because her husband, Ralph, was a volunteer fireman. "They're kept locked up, Mrs. Samios," she said. "There's a shack in the woods behind the firehouse. It's a little storage shack. They keep carnival prizes there and other seasonal things . . . But there's a padlock on the door! I don't know that anyone even knew the firecrackers were there!"

"They found 'em by accident," Bo said in a little voice. "Tina picked the lock. Yesterday."

"What do you know about picking locks!" Pa thundered at him.

"I don't! I don't!" Bo screeched. He pointed at Georgie, who had his head down. "That's what

.55.

Georgie said. It's just what he *said!* . . . What does it mean?"

"It means she managed to get the lock off the door," Pa said. "Did she tell you to steal the firecrackers?" he asked the twins.

"No," Georgie whispered. "She didn't care about the crackers. She liked the carnival stuff . . ."

"Did she take any of it?" I asked.

"Nah. But we played with it. They had these pop guns . . ." He stopped in the middle of the sentence and hung his head again. "Teddy and I went back later for the firecrackers. We know how to use 'em, Pop, honest! We were careful, we really were . . ."

Pa pulled Bo by the shoulders, away from Jessie. "Now you listen to me! Those things are against the law and there's a damn good reason for it! If one thing goes wrong or you don't know what you're doing you can be blinded for life! Or lose a finger! Or die! This isn't just some little kids' prank we're talking about, we're talking about lives!" Teddy and Georgie were staring at him with their mouths open. Then he turned to Bo. "Did you hear me? Isn't that what I've been telling you for years? Every time you ask for crackers?"

Bo nodded.

"We're going home," Pa said. "And you're going to bed early for a whole week!"

Bo started to yell. "NO! NO! I wanna see the show, please, I wanna see the show!" He hollered the entire way up the hill. Mr. and Mrs. Samios headed for the Shoreline, but the twins didn't say a word.

Ma turned to me. "I should make you go home, too, young lady," she said angrily.

"I'm sorry, Ma, I'm sorry. I only took my eyes off him for a second . . . It won't happen again . . ." I meant it. I was shaking.

The crowd that had gathered around Kozy Kabin was breaking up and the people were beginning to walk back to the beach area. As Ma turned away from me I saw someone behind her. It was a man, all by himself, carrying a blanket and a large flashlight. He had grown a beard but I recognized the walk right away. It was Mr. Hopper. He saw us and waved. I was glad he had arrived but I was too upset to wave back. I was scared to death over what might have happened to Bo and feeling very hurt about Tina. I didn't know why . . . It was like she had done something awful to me, personally. I looked down at my feet and saw that my toes were smeared with nail polish.

Chapter Five

But Bo didn't have to go to bed early for a week. Pa and Ma decided not to punish him that way for two reasons: one, he felt so bad about missing the fireworks show that he just moped around the whole next day, so they thought that might be enough punishment; and two, if Bo went to bed early, that'd mean I'd have to leave the restaurant with him and they really needed me down there. It seemed like this was going to be the busiest season *Punchy's* ever had, and I did a whole bunch of little things that nobody had the time to do. I made sure there was ice in the water pitchers, that the ashtrays were emptied, that the little lanterns Pa bought for each table all had working lightbulbs in them, that the napkins were all folded right, that there was no dried food left on the forks—stuff like that. Most of those jobs were the waiters' responsibilities, but Pa said it was hard to count on summer help who had their minds on seventeen-year-old blondes, even if they were local kids. And Bo helped, too. Ma had taught him how to load the dishwashers. So the business with the firecrackers was almost forgotten, except for one thing. Pa kept giving Bo lectures, almost hourly, on the way to behave with playmates.

It started the next morning, because it was Ma's breakfast shift.

"Bo Punch, sit down here."

Bo sat.

"Listen to me, young man, I don't care what your friends do, if you know something's wrong that they're doing, you *say* so, and you don't do it, you understand me?"

Bo nodded.

"Answer!"

"Yes sir."

"And if they do something that you know is dangerous, you go tell an adult so nobody ends up getting hurt. You got that?"

Nod from Bo.

"*Answer!*"

"Yes sir."

"Now that's not being a tattletale, that's being a good friend, because you could be saving them from some harm. Is that understood?"

"Yes sir."

Pa didn't really let up on Bo about that for a long time. While we were eating supper in the kitchen of the restaurant, Pa put down Bo's dessert and took his chin in his hand.

"You know, Bo," Pa said, "I was going to tell you not to play with those twins anymore . . ."

Bo sucked in his breath.

". . . but I know how much you like them, so I won't do that for now. But next time anything like this happens . . ."

"It won't, it won't, it won't," Bo wailed. "I'm sorry."

Pa mussed his hair and gave him his dessert.

Nobody said anything to Tina. I think Pa would have, he was just mad enough, but he was never there when she came around. I talked to her, though. I had to. I waited a few days because I just couldn't bring myself to start anything with her. It was bad enough whenever I said something accidentally that set her off. But finally, I spoke up because it bothered me too much.

"Hey, Tina?"

"What?"

"Was it true you picked the lock on the firemen's shack?" I asked.

"Who toldja that?"

"Georgie," I answered.

She smiled. "I just showed the kids how to do it. It's easy with a bobby pin. I didn't mean for them to take anything, though."

We were lying on the grass under the willow tree in our back yard. I reached up and pulled down one of the branches that was close to my head. "You know, those kids could have been killed. That was really a dumb thing to do, and besides it's against the law."

"You sound like old Harris," she said, pulling down her own branch. "Anyway, I told you, I didn't make them steal the stuff."

"But they're only little kids!" I said. "Sure they're going to take firecrackers when they see them lying there like that. Bo's been wanting firecrackers since he was about four!"

Tina rolled over on her side and propped up her head with her hand. "You know what my mother's going to bring me back from Spain? A real bullfighter's cape. A red one, made out of silk. Do you think they have girl bullfighters yet?"

"Tina—"

"I betcha I'd be great. I wouldn't be afraid if a bull came right at me. All you do is swish that cape and dodge right out of the way."

I sighed. "Is your mother in Spain?" I asked.

"Sure. She's all over. She doesn't stay in one place. She's going to Africa, too." She began to throw pebbles against the trunk of the tree.

"Does she send you picture postcards?" I wanted to know. "Can I see them?"

"No, she doesn't send postcards," Tina answered, making me feel silly for asking. "She sends letters. Long ones, on airmail stationery. She can't say everything she wants to on a postcard. Hey, don't you have to feed the kids lunch or something?"

"Yeah . . . but, Tina?" I still had to find out about the lock business. And the stealing.

"What? Come on, let's go eat," she said, getting up.

"When you showed the kids how to pick the lock on the shack—"

"Oh, jeez—"

"No, wait, just answer this—" I really wanted to know what she had been thinking. "Wasn't it just a trick you were showing them? I mean, you didn't *mean* for them to steal . . . or get hurt or anything. Right?"

"Oh, I don't know, S.J. What difference does it make? I didn't want 'em to get hurt. Come on, I'll race you back!"

As I started to run after her, I thought—it's okay. She was just showing them how to get a lock open. That was all. She just didn't think it out.

A couple of mornings later, Pa called from the restaurant. It seemed that Mr. Sumner, over at the gas station, had three jobs going at once and having only Travis for a mechanic wasn't enough. He asked Pa if he could borrow Earl to help out for that morning. So Pa called and asked if he could borrow *me*, to help *him* out for that morning.

"Have you ever waited table before, Sarajane?" Mama asked as I quickly dressed.

"Sure, don't you remember last Labor Day weekend? I worked lunches, two days."

"You were a busgirl, Sarajane."

"No, no, I waited. I even got tipped. Don't you remember?" I took a rubber band and pulled my hair back into a pony tail. It's not good to wear long hair down when you wait on tables, it can get into the food. You can't have a lady pulling hair out of her soup!

"You're right," Ma said, "I forgot. You were a big help. Now you're older, you'll be a bigger help. Get on down there."

I was kind of excited. See, the customers don't care how young you are. They just want their food, so they give their order to you like they would to any real waitress and they expect you to fill it. I found out, if a man buys lemonade from you at a stand, he pats you on the head and thinks it's cute. But if he's sitting at a table in a restaurant and he's hungry, you could be four years old, but if you ask him what he wants and you're holding a pencil and pad, he'll give it to you fast, right down to dressing-and-hold-the-onions.

.63.

I headed right for the kitchen.

"Pa, there are a lot of people there!" I said, surprised.

"There's a good number," he said, nodding. "I knew I was right and this was a good idea. Your mama finally agreed with me . . ."

"I know. What station should I take?" I didn't have a real uniform, so I had worn a denim skirt and white blouse. Ma had made a pretty apron for me, embroidered with the lily-of-the-valley flowers I drew and I kept that in the kitchen and put it on when I needed it. I quickly tied its sash.

"Station One," Pa said. "Scotty can handle the rest. It won't be hard, honey. Breakfast doesn't have that big a menu."

"Hi, Sarajane," Katie called from the stove, where she was scrambling eggs into a frying pan. She went to the restaurant with whoever opened up, every morning now.

"Hi, Kate. Busy, huh?"

"You bet. Want an omelet?" she called.

"Family eats last," Pa said. "Now go on out there and see to tables two and three."

There were two women and two little girls at table two. They were all dressed up, with lots of makeup so I knew they were summer people. Anyway, I didn't know them.

"May I take your order, ma'am?" I asked, the way I was taught. I held my pencil up and my pad ready.

One of the women was talking. She just glanced at

me. "Just a minute, Miss. So anyway, I told Marjorie she couldn't possibly have the week off, even though we were taking the children, there was just still so much to be done around the house!"

"Well, I don't know, Alice," the other one said. "I can't imagine what there is to do around that place when no one's there, really." She looked up at me. "Dear, the girl is waiting for our order."

The woman called Alice picked up her menu. "Oh, I don't know . . . what're *you* having, Nora?"

"Oh . . . I don't know."

"I want Eggs Benedict," one of the little girls piped up. "Chilled grapefruit juice first." I figured she was around eight.

"Sorry, that's not on the menu," I said, and began to read the choice of eggs to her.

She made a clicking sound with her tongue. "I can *read*," she said.

"Miss, can you come back in a few minutes?" Alice asked.

"Yes, ma'am," I was glad to say, and I beat it over to table three.

What a relief! Mr. Hopper was at table three. He was all by himself, studying the menu.

"Hi, Mr. Hopper. May I help you?" I smiled and held up my pad and pencil.

He put down his menu. "Well, this can't be little Sarajane Punch, all grown up and waiting on tables," he said and smiled back.

"Yeah, and I'm sure glad to be waiting on this one.

The one over there isn't too friendly," I said, nodding at table two.

"Ah, too bad," he said. "Well, I'll make it up to you by being extra friendly this morning. What would you like me to order?"

I laughed. "I'm supposed to ask *you* that."

"Yes, but this is a new menu. *Punchy's* hasn't been open for breakfast before, if memory serves, and I must learn the house specialties. What do you recommend?"

"Oh, you know everything's good at *Punchy's*," I said. "But my sister makes — uh — I mean, the omelets are very good . . ."

"Fine, well, bring me a cheese omelet. And orange juice and coffee." He handed me his menu. "And thank you very much, Sarajane."

"You're welcome." I wrote the order down. "Hey, I like your beard. I mean . . . it looks nice."

Mr. Hopper touched it with the tips of his fingers. "Thank you," he smiled. "I think you're the only one who noticed I grew one!" and he laughed.

"Aw no," I said. "Anyway, it makes you look like a writer."

"Good," he answered. "At least I can look like one."

"Mr. Hopper?"

"Hm?"

"Do you have a lot of new stories to try out on us this year?"

He didn't answer right away. He just looked at me. It was almost as if he hadn't heard what I asked him. But after a while he said, "Yes. Of course I do. Lots. We'll see you soon."

"Okay," I said, and turned to get his order to the kitchen.

"Sarajane?" he called.

I came back. "Yessir?"

"Listen, your brother's all right, isn't he? I mean, the other day, with the firecrackers—"

"Oh. Thanks, he's fine."

"Well, good," Mr. Hopper said. "You be sure to bring him along for the stories, all right?"

"'Course I will." I brought the order in to Pa and Katie and went back to table two.

"Ma'am?" I said to Alice.

"Oh, yes," she said, "you certainly did take your time. Now *she* will have tomato juice," (she pronounced it to-MAH-to) "a three-minute egg, and a glass of milk. I will have dry wheat toast and coffee."

"Yes, ma'am." I nodded at the other lady who spoke for herself and *her* little girl.

"We'll just have orange juice, French toast, milk for her and tea for me. Thank you."

"Welcome," I said, and turned away. I liked the second lady better.

The breakfast shift ended at ten. Usually Pa or Ma went out back where they relaxed on a hammock we had strung up between the trees, or home for a quick nap before lunch. But with Earl out, Pa stayed to clean up with Katie. I went home to watch Bo so Ma could go down and help them. She was faster and better than I was at cleaning up.

"How was it?" she asked as I walked in.

"Fine," I said. "It was easy!"

Ma began to laugh. "Easy! Waiting tables is easy?"

I tilted my head at her. "Sure, it's easy. Why?"

"Well, honey, I'm glad you enjoyed it. I hope you go on enjoying it, but—"

"But what?"

"*But*, after you've been on your feet through two or three shifts, put up with some nasty customers, collected a whole dollar-thirty in tips . . . Oh, pay no attention to me, Sara. It's just a little harder as you get older. Anyway, you were a big help and we appreciate it. Now look, you've still got your apron on. Untie it and I'll take it back with me."

I handed it to her and she left, after telling me what to give Bo for lunch. I never could eat what he ate. He had stuff like cold cereal, dry with no milk, and toast with jam, but no butter. Or he'd have plain peanut butter sandwiches without jam, so there was nothing to keep it from gluing your mouth together for the rest of the day. I had real-people lunches, but Bo ate weird.

Ma wasn't even down the block two minutes when Tina came in, without knocking, through the kitchen door. The twins were with her but they didn't come in. They ran around to the back where Bo was swinging on his tire swing.

"Hey, that's pretty. I never saw you in a dress before," I told her. Actually, it looked kind of funny on her. She just didn't seem the dress type. "Except you still have the dumb red circles on your knees."

"They're there on *purpose*," she said. "I *want* 'em there."

"Are you going somewhere?" I asked.

"Yeah, I'm going somewhere," she sang at me. "Some place *you'd* like to go, I bet. New York City."

"Sure, I'd like that," I told her. "I've only been there a couple of times. And so long ago I can hardly remember. What are you going to do there?"

She stuck out her jaw like she was going to say something mean, but she didn't. "I'm not even sure what we'll do," she said. "My mother told the Harrises that if I were allowed to stay with them, that they had to plan terrific things for me to do so I wouldn't get bored. And there's lots to do in the city. You wouldn't believe it!"

"That was nice of your mother," I said.

"Bet your basket," Tina said.

"When are you leaving?"

"Oh, just about now," she answered. "I just wanted to let you know I wouldn't be around today, in case you were looking for me."

"Yeah, thanks," I said.

Tina stopped at the door. "Maybe I'll bring you back something from the Big Apple," she said. "You know, that's what New Yorkers call the city."

"What'll you bring me back?" I asked.

"Maybe a big worm!" she said and laughed. I was still shaking my head at her after she slammed out the door.

Right after lunch, just as I was about to take Bo and the twins to the lake, the phone rang. It was Ma, calling from the restaurant.

"Sarajane, Mrs. Harris came by this morning and she asked me if you could go to their cabin for supper tonight and sleep over with Tina."

"She *did*?"

"Yes. Why do you sound so surprised? You've done that sorta thing before."

"I—know—but, I mean, Tina was here this morning. She didn't ask me any of that. And she said she was going to New York for the day."

"Well, she is," Mama said. "But when they come back. Mrs. Harris thought that would be nice. It was her idea, she was going to surprise Tina."

"Oh."

"Well? Do you want to? I told her I couldn't say yes till I talked to you."

"Oh."

"Well, *do* you? Come on, I've got to get back to work."

I thought. "Well, I can't go for supper. You need me to help down there."

There was a short pause. "Well . . . it'd be all right this once if you want to go," she said.

"You sure?" I asked. I wasn't sure I wanted to.

"Yes, Sarajane, now what is it? I've got to plan here!"

"Okay, okay!" I said quickly. "I'll go."

Chapter Six

I was nervous all day. Being with Tina during the daytime was strange enough! What would it be like for a night?

At five-thirty, I brought Bo and Katie down to the restaurant, where Ma had their suppers waiting.

"Don't you want me to do a little work first before I go?" I wanted to know. "I mean can you really do without me tonight? We've been so busy . . ."

But Ma just rubbed my cheek with her hand. "Run along, Sarajane, we'll be all right."

"But—"

"Go *on* now, you'll be late. Have a good time."

I stood there. "Don't you want me to just fold the napkins? Earl still doesn't do it right . . ."

"Earl does it *fine*," Ma said and started for the kitchen. Then she stopped. "Sara," she said, walking back toward me, "don't you want to go? Is that it?"

Yes. No. I don't know, I thought. What I said was, "I just know how much help you need, is all."

"We'll make it. For tonight. Go on along," she said, and this time stayed to watch me leave.

I took a long time walking to the Shoreline. I kicked three rocks, all the way there; had to go back and kick each one to keep up with the others. When I got all three rocks plus myself to the wooden gate of the Harrises' cabin, I decided I should have kicked maybe *five*.

Tina opened the door before I even knocked. She had changed out of her dress.

"Hi," I said.

"Yeah?" from Tina.

"How was the Big Apple? What'd you do there?" I asked.

She turned her head around and looked inside the cabin. Then she stepped out on the porch. "Wanna go for a walk?" she said.

"Well . . . aren't we gonna eat now? My mother said Mrs. Harris said quarter to six."

"It's not ready yet," Tina said. "Let's walk around."

"Well . . ." I felt funny. "Shouldn't I tell your—I mean Mrs. Harris I'm here?"

Tina stepped off the porch. "Oh, never mind!" she said. "Go on in and tell her, Miss Priss, I'm going for a walk!"

I heaved a big sigh. Out loud. "Oh, all *right*," I said, hoping it was loud enough for Mrs. Harris to know I was there. "I'm coming, wait up."

We began to head toward the lake. "You gonna stay for the night or just for dinner?" Tina asked.

"The night!" I said. "Otherwise what would I be doing with this?" I jerked my head at my shoulder bag which had my change of clothes and toothbrush in it.

"You mean . . ." she said, half closing her eyes, "you're really going to . . . spend the night? Not just go home after dinner?"

"I thought I just said that," I told her.

"Yeah, but . . . you want to? Or did Emily make you?" she said.

"Nobody *makes* me spend the night," I said. "Besides, I didn't even talk to Mrs. Harris. My mother just said she invited me. Anyway I thought I was supposed to be a surprise. How come you were expecting me?"

Tina bent down and pulled up a handful of weeds. "Ah, she's so stupid . . . If she was gonna make a surprise, why'd she set *four* places at the table, when there's only three of us? She's so dumb . . ."

I didn't say, don't call her dumb or stupid, she was trying to do something nice for you! I wanted to say it, but I didn't say it.

"Tina!" It was Mrs. Harris, calling from the cabin. "Tee-na!"

Tina kept walking.

"Come on, Tina," I said, pulling on her sleeve. "She's calling. Supper's ready. Come on . . ."

"It's *only* spaghetti and meatballs," Tina said.

"Who cares *what* it is?" I said. "Besides, I *love* spaghetti and meatballs! Hey, let's *go*!"

"Oh, all right," Tina grumbled. "But only because *you're* here. Otherwise I'd keep on going. Know what I did in the city?"

"What?"

"Went to the zoo. *And* the Empire State Building. *And* on a ferry boat. *And* to a fancy restaurant. Fancier than yours!"

"There are plenty of restaurants fancier," I said, "but the food's no better anywhere."

"Howda *you* know?" she said as we arrived at the gate. "You've never been anywhere."

I felt like I was going to cry. I might have, too, but Tina suddenly stopped and pulled on *my* sleeve. "Hey, S.J. . . ."

"What?"

"Uh—don't tell Jim and Emily about the—about what I told you," she said.

"What did you tell me?" I didn't know what she was talking about.

"Don't tell them . . . that I told you what we did in New York, okay? They'd think I was bragging.

.75.

They hate that. So don't talk about it, okay? Okay?"

"Okay!" I said. "Okay!"

We got through dinner. It was real good. Not as good as Mama's, of course, but good. Mr. and Mrs. Harris talked a lot, mostly to me, because Tina didn't say a word. She didn't even stay at the table for dessert, which was Breyer's Natural Mint Ice Cream, my favorite, next to the peach ice cream we make ourselves in August. So I stayed and ate it.

"Don't mind Tina, Sarajane," Mrs. Harris said, touching my arm. "Sometimes . . . when she's not feeling too good, she—she gets angry. It's just her way, you mustn't—you know, take it personally, or anything."

"Uh huh," I said.

"Really," Mrs. Harris said. "She likes you. Very much. That's why we invited you over. We thought . . ."

"We thought if anyone could make her feel better, you could," Mr. Harris finished.

Boy, I thought, if she likes me very much, I'd sure wouldn't want to be anyone she hated!

"Guess I haven't done a very good job," I said to them.

"Oh, honey," Mrs. Harris said, "she'll get over her mood. She'll be all right, you'll see. Finish your ice cream."

I already had.

Mrs. Harris wouldn't let me help with the dishes. I got up right away, like I always do, and started to scrape, stack and wash, but she just grabbed a dish right out of my hand. "You go and find Tina, Sarajane. I'll do this. Listen, I think I hear her in her room."

"Oh . . . but . . . first I'll do the dishes," I said, trying to get the dish back. I wasn't used to this.

"Please," Mrs. Harris said firmly. "Go stay with Tina. Mr. Harris will help me with the dishes. Sarajane . . . you're a very nice girl."

"Thank you," I said, and went to hunt up Tina's room. It sure felt funny to just get up and leave the table without doing something. I mean, sometimes Katie did the dishes, but that was because I had some other kind of work to do.

It wasn't hard finding Tina's room. There were only two bedrooms in the cabin. The door to one was closed and I could see there was no one in the other. I knocked.

"Hey, Tina? C'n I come in?"

No answer.

"Tina? Hey!" I knocked again.

"Oh, just come in!" she yelled. "Quit that pounding!"

"I don't get you," I said, stepping into the room.

"Close the door!" she snapped. I did. It was made of barn wood, just like the rest of the room. In fact, so was the whole cabin. Rough barn wood. It was nice, but kind of dark. Tina's room was small and square, with a window on one wall that overlooked the lake. I noticed the screen was torn. They should fix it, I thought, or tell Mr. Samios. It gets really buggy around the lake, especially in late July.

"What don't you *get*?" Tina sneered.

"Oh. I don't get why you're in such a bad mood, when you had such a neat day!"

"Didn't I ask you not to talk about it?" she said.

"You said not to talk about it to the Harrises," I told her. "And I didn't."

"Well, don't talk about it to me, either," she said and flopped down on the bed on her back.

"You want me to go home?" I asked, praying she would say yes. I knew I couldn't go unless she told me to. I had a feeling I'd be letting down the Harrises.

Tina sat up quickly. "No. You going?"

"You sure you don't want me to?"

"Yeah. You going anyway?"

I shook my head. Tina flopped back down.

"Hey," I began, "you want to do something? *Now* we could go for a walk. Or play cards or something . . ."

"Know how to play poker?" Tina asked grinning at me.

"Oh, sure!" I grinned back. "I can beat my pa!"

"You can?"

"You bet!"

"What else is there to do?" Tina asked.

I couldn't think of anything. In the summer, I was always busy working after dinner. Sometimes in the winter, too, but usually there was homework or TV.

I never watched TV in the summer and the cabin didn't even have one.

"Listen," I said. "Wanna go over to the restaurant and help out? It's only a quarter to seven . . . We could probably bus or something . . ."

"What's 'bus'?"

"You know, clean up the tables when the people are through."

"Oh, boy, you sure know how to have fun," she said.

"It *is* fun, kinda," I said. "Come on. It'll be something different for you."

"You think your father'll let me?" she asked. "Nah, forget it."

"Sure he will. They're *busy*," I told her. I stood up before she could say no again. "I'll tell the Harrises. Okay?"

She got up. "Yeah, okay," she said.

The Harrises seemed glad about it. We ran all the way. I didn't kick one rock.

We went in through the back door. Pa and Ma and Katie were all sweating and the noise from the dining room told me just how crowded it was. Earl and Scotty dashed in and dashed out. Everyone looked surprised to see us, but when I said we came to help, Ma just said "Good" and threw aprons at us. "Tina, you just go out there and watch Sara. She'll show you what to do, it's easy. And," she smiled, "thanks a lot!"

Before we knew it it was nine o'clock. When Tina and I came into the kitchen with another tray full of dirty dishes, Mama said, "That's it, girls. You did a wonderful job. Go on back to Tina's and get some rest. The big load's over."

Tina wiped her forehead with her apron. "There's still some people out there, Mrs. Punch," she said.

"It's all right, honey. We can manage. You were just fine!" Ma smiled at her.

"Yeah?"

"Yeah," Ma said. "Go home."

Neither of us said anything as we walked home in the dark.

The Harrises were sitting on the porch of their cabin when we got there. I was so tired I was ready to go right to bed and hoped Tina was, too. But Mr. Harris stood up as we got near and stopped us.

"Wait a minute, girls," he said, "I've got something to show you. A surprise." He had a big lantern and we followed him around the cabin to a little clearing, where we saw he had set up a canvas tent.

"Thought you might enjoy camping out," he said, smiling. "I've got two sleeping bags in there and you two can have some privacy. How's that?" he asked, looking right at Tina.

She had her head tilted and was looking at the tent. "What if something crawls in it?" she asked.

"Hey, I've camped out lots of times," I said, "*without* a tent. It's fun. Really. Don't be scared."

"Who's scared," she growled at me.

"Well . . . if you'd like to wash up first in the cabin . . ." Mr. Harris said.

"Sure," I said, taking the lantern from him. "And we don't have to change into pajamas, either. We stay in our clothes when we sleep outside." We went back to the cabin and all I took out of my bag was my toothbrush. I washed and Tina went into her room and closed the door.

When I was finished, I called her. No answer, so I knocked on the door.

"Just a minute, willya?" she called, so I stood there and waited. Finally, she came out and we headed back to the tent.

"Have fun!" Mrs. Harris called.

"G'night!" I called back. Tina didn't say anything.

We crawled into the tent and right into the sleeping bags without a word. I was exhausted, like I usually was at night. Ma said sometimes I was asleep before my head hit the pillow. She might be right, because lots of times I can't remember even getting undressed. Tonight is one of those nights, I thought.

"I'm so tired," I said, softly. "Is it okay if we don't talk now?"

"Yeah, who wants to talk," Tina said and rolled over.

"Well . . . g'night," I said. She didn't answer, or if she did I don't remember because I was out.

The voices woke me. There were two voices, practically right in my ear. They were having a conversation, quietly, but not whispering, either. I opened one eye and got scared because I couldn't remember where I was. Then I saw that I was facing a sleeping bag and it came back to me. But the voices . . . they were Tina's. Both voices were Tina's, at least they were both coming from the same person's mouth. One of them was Tina's regular voice that I knew, but the other . . . the other was, I don't know, deeper? Not deeper, exactly, but—different. Like a grownup sounds when he or she is talking to a child. Anyway, it wasn't like Tina usually sounds, that was for sure.

I knew that I shouldn't move. I just felt I couldn't let her know I was awake, so I quickly closed my eyes and just listened.

" . . . thinks he knows everything," Tina's own voice said.

"You know he's only trying to help, dear," the other voice replied. It sounded . . . soothing. Nice.

"He's *no* help," Tina said "Nobody ever helps. Just *you* . . ."

You who, I wondered? I opened one eye again just the littlest bit, trying to glimpse *something* through my eyelashes without disturbing her. She was lying on her side, facing me. But she wasn't looking at me, she was looking at something in her hand. I squinted even more, if that was possible, and picked up a kind of glittering. It was a chain, and it was reflecting lights from the moon and the lantern, through the slit in the tent. The lights were flickering across my sleeping bag because Tina was holding something on the end of the chain and everytime she talked, the chain moved.

"Nobody *really* likes me," Tina continued, "they only pretend they do. But I can tell." She clutched whatever was on the end of the chain tighter and held it up to her cheek.

Then the other voice answered her. "Maybe you don't give people a chance," it said. "Maybe you should have more faith in people, honey. Lots of people are kind . . ."

"You sound just like *him*," Tina said back to the other voice. "You know what he said today?"

The other voice said, "What?"

"Oh, forget it. I was mean to S.J. . . . and I didn't want to be . . ."

Soothingly, the other voice said, "That was only because you were angry, dear. Sometimes you're so angry that you take it out on other people . . ."

"Well, I can't help it," Tina said, and her voice broke. She put the chain-thing up to her lips and began to make little whimpering noises. I closed my eyes.

Finally, the whimpering stopped and Tina talked again. "You know what?" she said. "When I saw the buildings in New York from the car window this morning, I got sick to my stomach."

"I know," the other voice said, like a kind, calm grownup. "I know, dear."

I heard a funny sound. I peeked again and saw that Tina was rocking back and forth.

"He says I'm lucky," she said. "He says this is the best place of all. Do you think so? Do you think this is the best place of all?"

But this time, the other voice didn't answer her. I mean, she didn't answer in the other voice.

"Who would care if I died?" Tina whispered to the chain-thing next to her lips.

"Lots of people would care," the other voice said. "You know that . . . you know that."

I thought, if the other voice were a real person it would be hugging Tina now. "I *hate* going to New York," Tina said, and then, quickly, "No, I don't."

There was a long pause. I didn't hear the chain-thing answer. Just when I was beginning to think Tina had finally fallen asleep, I heard her say again, "*Is* this really the best place of all?" And then, nothing more.

I was wide awake. I couldn't have gone to sleep then if I'd just worked ten night shifts in a row! I listened to make sure Tina's breathing was slow and regular, like Katie's was when she slept, and then I felt I could stretch out. My whole side hurt, where I'd been lying so stiff, trying not to move. I wanted to see, *had* to see what Tina had been talking to. *With*. I sat up. Tina was lying on her left arm, still facing my sleeping bag. Her right thumb was almost in her mouth. The chain-thing was in her hand, close to me. But all I could see was the chain. Whatever was on the end was clutched in her fist.

I began to feel tears starting and I bit down on the quilting of the sleeping bag.

Chapter Seven

When I woke up the next morning, Tina's sleeping bag was empty and I didn't hear any noises, except the usual ones from the lake. I could tell by the way the sun was shining that it was later than usual . . . I must have been really tired to oversleep like that.

I called softly, "Tina?" but got no answer. Then all of a sudden I remembered what had kept me up. The voices—the two different Tinas—

My stomach started to jump around and I didn't feel hungry like I usually do when I first wake up. She had a chain . . . with something on the end of it . . .

I looked over at her sleeping bag but nothing was there. Then I did something I hated myself for, but I just couldn't help it. I didn't even give myself time to think about it. I reached over and lifted up the pillow at the head of her sleeping bag. There was nothing there and I felt both glad and sorry. I lay back on my own pillow and tried to think about what to do, how to act, what to say . . .

That other voice . . . the grownup-sounding one. Who was it supposed to be? Tina spoke to it like she never spoke to me.

"Hey, S.J.! You gonna sleep all day?" from outside the tent.

"Tina?" I sat up.

"No, it's Mr. Spock. Who else would it be!" She lifted the tent flap and crawled in. "I've been waiting to eat breakfast for an hour. Get up, I'm starving!"

"What time is it?"

"Nine. Almost nine. Come on!"

I unzipped part of the bag and got up. Then I started to fold and roll up the bag.

"Just leave that stuff, willya?" she said, pulling at me. "I said I'm starving! Besides, we might as well just leave it here. We'll be using it again."

I looked at her. This was the Tina I was used to. There was no chain around her neck . . . "Okay," I said. "Tina."

"What?"

"Uh . . . Did you sleep okay?"

"Sure!"

"Good . . . me, too."

We went back to her cabin, where Emily had made French toast, and I started to get my hunger back.

"Want more, honey?" Mrs. Harris asked me. Tina was already on her seconds.

"No, thanks. Did Mr. Harris eat already?"

"Oh, sure, he was gone by six-thirty. See, the shift he's on starts at eight o'clock, but he has to be there a half-hour before that, so he's got to leave here six-thirty the latest."

"Oh."

"He's a patrolman . . ." she said.

"Uh huh . . ."

"See, there are different shifts—he's on the eight-to-four this week . . . Did you sleep all right, Sarajane?" I looked up at her. She asked *me* the question, but she was looking right at Tina, who was still eating. For a minute I wasn't sure if I was supposed to answer. But then she turned and looked at me.

"Oh, yes ma'am," I said. "Fine." Then we both looked at Tina. "I didn't hear a *thing*!" I said, after a pause, and then I got scared that maybe that sounded funny, so I said, "I mean, I slept like a rock!" Tina still paid no attention. I wondered if Tina had talked in that other voice before at night, and if Mrs. Harris had heard her.

"I really have to go," I said, picking up my dishes. "I have to see what's happening at home . . . I have work to do . . . you know."

"Thanks for coming, Sarajane," Mrs. Harris said.

"Thank you very much for having me," I remembered to say. "I had a real good time."

"Pleasure."

"Hey, S.J. Catch you later, okay?" Tina said.

"Sure." I smiled at her. "It was fun, Tina."

"Oh, yeah . . ." she said. "Yeah."

Ma was there when I got home. It was Pa's breakfast shift, and I was really glad. I wanted to talk to her. I mean, Pa's really great, but it's always been that when I have a problem, Mama's the one I like to talk to. She had just turned on the sprinkler for Bo and I met her at the kitchen door.

"Oh, honey, I thought you'd be back before this. Everything okay?" she asked.

"Uh huh."

"Well . . . come on in and you can tell me about it." She opened the screen door for me and followed me in. "Want to thank you for last night," she said. "You two girls were a big help. I think Tina kind of enjoyed it, don't you?"

"I think so." I sat down at the table and looked at the placemat. It was Bo's. White and orange in the shape of a kitten. I ran my finger around the edge a few times. When I finally looked up, I saw Ma was standing there just watching me.

I laughed. "I thought you were doing something," I said.

"I was. Watching you trace the placemat." She sat

down next to me. "How was it last night? Was it fun?"

"Yeah . . . Ma?"

"What?"

"You know . . . people are funny."

Ma threw her head back and laughed. "Yes, that's true, that's true!" she said. "That what you learned last night?"

"Maybe . . . Maybe people aren't really what you think they are. I mean from the way they act."

"You can't always tell about people from the way they act," Ma said. "What 'people' did you have in mind?"

I didn't answer.

"You thinking of Tina?" she asked and I nodded. "Sarajane, how much do you know about Tina?"

I shook my head. "Not very much," I said. "I think less now than I did before."

"Why do you say that?" Ma asked.

"Oh, I don't know." I didn't want to tell about the chain-thing. In fact, I didn't want to say anything very much about Tina. I had a feeling everything I knew was supposed to be a secret, but I couldn't say why. Tina never said that the things she told me were secrets but I wanted to keep them that way for her anyway.

"Sarajane, do you know what a foster child is?"

"A what?" I stared at Ma.

"A foster child. Did you ever hear of that before?"

"Uh, I don't think so."

"Well, when Mrs. Harris called yesterday . . . Remember? To ask me if you could sleep over?"

"Yes . . ."

"The reason I let you go, let you out of work and everything, was because of some of the things Mrs. Harris told me. See, Tina is a foster child. She's living with the Harrises now, but she's lived with other families before them."

"No, she's just staying with them. For the summer. While her mother's . . . um . . away," I explained. Ma must have heard wrong.

"No, see, honey—her mother couldn't keep her. At home. So she got in touch with the Child Welfare League and the Department of Social Services and they were able to find a home . . . some homes for her. And the reason Mrs. Harris called was, yesterday was Tina's day to visit her case worker. That's a person from the Department of Social Services who looks after some of these children."

"Tina went to the Empire State Building!" I blurted out.

"No, Sarajane, Tina was taken by the Harrises to visit her case worker, so that he could check up on her and see how she was making out with her new family. And the reason Mrs. Harris wanted you over last night was, Tina sometimes gets nightmares before and after she sees the case worker, and Mrs. Harris thought it might help if you were there. She never told you any of this? No, I guess not. The Empire State Building, huh?"

I nodded.

"Well, maybe it's good you know. It'll be less confusing for you. Did she have any nightmares last night?"

I shook my head no. It wasn't a lie. Nightmares are things you have when you're sleeping. I don't know what you call them when you're awake.

"What about the other families she lived with?" I asked.

"Oh, I don't know about them," Mama answered. "I only know that Mrs. Harris said that she and her husband weren't the first that Tina's been with. I guess the others just didn't work out for some reason. Anyway, when she explained why she wanted you, I thought it might be a good thing if you went. And you could use the time off." She smiled. "Besides, I really didn't think you disliked the girl."

"I don't," I said. "I just can't figure her. Why didn't you tell me before?"

Ma leaned back in her chair. "Well . . . I wasn't sure you didn't know, for one thing, though I should have guessed . . . And for another, I figured that maybe if I told you, you'd act differently toward Tina."

"What do you mean, differently?" I wanted to know.

"Well, sometimes when you know a secret about someone, your behavior toward them changes. You're a little afraid to act natural, you know? You think maybe they'll find out you *know*, and you get so nervous, they find out anyway. Know what I mean?"

I frowned at the floor. "Maybe . . ." I said.

"Anyway, if Tina wants her background to be a secret, then it should be one. For now. You just go on being her friend. Maybe she'll tell you about it herself some time."

My head was spinning around. The case worker . . . that explained why Tina went to New York and why she was unhappy about it . . . Did that mean that Tina's mother *wasn't* traveling around Europe then? Or maybe that's why she couldn't keep Tina. And what about the uncle who owned a department store?

"Ma? Did Mrs. Harris say why Tina's mother couldn't keep her?" I asked.

"No, she didn't, Sarajane. You know all I know right now."

"Okay," I nodded. "Guess that explains some of it . . ."

"It's awful hard to be handed around from foster family to foster family," Ma said. "Sometimes makes kids act pretty angry . . . do some mean things . . ."

I nodded again. "Yeah. Oh, yeah."

"They're never sure where they really belong. And they're always thinking about their own family, I bet," Ma said.

"You can't always tell about people from the way they act," I repeated like it was a school lesson. "You sure can't. What do I do now?"

"Now?" Ma asked, getting up." Now you see if

Bo's sheets are wet and then come down and help me shell peas!"

"Oh, Ma . . ."

Ma and I worked around the house until just before it was time for her to leave for the lunch shift. Tina showed up, just as she was getting ready to go. As usual, she didn't knock.

"Hey, S.J.!" *Slam* went the screen door!

"Hey, Tina!"

"Hi, there," Ma said. "You did fine last night. Thanks."

Tina didn't say anything, just looked at her. She tilted her head to one side.

"What's the matter," Ma said, "don't you believe me? I mean it. I didn't expect to see you and Sarajane last night, but I don't know how we would have managed without you."

Tina shrugged. "Oh . . . well . . ." She turned her back to us both and walked toward the table. "I could probably find the time to do it again . . . I mean . . . if you needed the help I guess I could probably . . ." she shrugged again and began to play with the spoon in the sugar bowl.

"Well!" Ma said. "How about right now?"

Tina whirled around. "*Now?*"

"Why not?" Ma said. "Let's go. Big lunch shift." Tina just stood there. "Well?"

"Not S.J.?" Tina asked.

"No, she's got to keep Bo happy this afternoon. Just you, lady. Make up your mind, I'm on my way out."

Another shrug from Tina. "Okay, sure," she said. A wave to me. "See ya."

I nodded. As the door opened and they went out, I yelled, "Oh, hey, Tina, you better tell the—" *Slam* went the door. I went over to it. "—Harrises where you'll be!"

She didn't even turn around. "Oh, I'll do it when I take Bo swimming," I mumbled and turned back into the kitchen.

Chapter Eight

After that, Tina began to work a lot at the restaurant, even without me. Everybody seemed happy about
it except Katie, who grumbled a bit, but she really
didn't have much to do with Tina, who was busing,
mostly. Even Pa was impressed. "She can really heft
those trays!" he said, raising his eyebrows. "Full of
dishes and everything! She's strong for a—"

"*Girl?*" Ma said, playfully raising her fist.

"*Little* girl," Pa said.

"Sarajane does better," Katie muttered.

"No. I don't," I said. I'd been there a few times

with Tina, dinners mostly, because that's what I worked. "She *is* strong, and she's good."

"I've been paying her something each time she works," Pa said, "but she's been making some pretty good tips. At least I think she has. She comes into the kitchen griping about some cheapskate who only left her a quarter . . ." he chuckled. "She should know busboys aren't usually tipped at all. At least at *Punchy's* . . ."

"Bus*girl*," Ma and I said together and laughed.

"Anyway, she probably gets tips because folks see that she is a small girl doing what used to be a strong boy's job. And doing it well. She deserves good tips," Ma said.

"Do you *mind* if we don't discuss Tina Gogo any more tonight?" Katie asked. "I never heard anybody talked about so much in this house!" And that ended *that* conversation.

On Saturdays, I helped on the lunch shift. Bo played in the kitchen or outside and we took turns watching him. Sometimes, he even stacked the dishes.

One Saturday, the lunch hour was so busy, that when it was over, Ma sent me down to the lake by myself for a swim and a rest before the supper shift. I was sunning myself, half-dozing, when I felt a glob of water on my right foot. I opened my eyes. Mr. Hopper was standing over me with an empty bucket. He was laughing.

"What a life!" he said, shaking his head. "Wish

I were a kid, with a whole summer to goof off! Aren't you the lazy one!"

I picked up a handful of sand and threw it at him. "Are you kidding?" I yelled. "Goofing off! You wanna know what I did *today* . . ."

"Wait a *minute!*" he cried, holding up his hands to block my sand attack, "*W*a*it* a minute! I'm kidding, I'm kidding!" He sat down next to me. "You know darn well, *I'm* the one who's up here goofing off. *You're* the worker. There's some kind of irony in that, don't you think?"

"I don't know what you mean," I said, "but aren't you up here to write? Jessie told Ma something about a book . . . *That's* work, isn't it?"

He stopped laughing and closed his eyes. "Yah," he said quickly. "That's work."

"Hey, Mr. Hopper?"

"Hm?"

"You haven't had one night of stories since you been here. Aren't you gonna do it this year?"

His smile came back. "Sure," he said. "You bet. One night real soon. I'll let you know, okay?"

"Okay."

I got back early for the supper shift and Tina was already there. So were the Harrises. They were all in the kitchen with Pa and Ma and Katie and Bo.

"Know who I saw at the beach?" I said to everyone.

"Robinson Crusoe," Tina said.

"No," I said, "it was—"

"Jaws!" Tina yelled.

"No, for Pete's sake, it was Mr. Hopper!"

"Thrilling," Tina said, and went over to watch Ma cut out melon balls.

"Naw, he's nice. Anyway, he said he's going to have a story night soon. Real soon."

Katie turned around. "Oh, that's great!" she said.

"When, when?" Bo asked, jumping up. "Tonight?"

"No, not tonight," Mama answered him. "But soon."

"Boy, that's the most exciting news since Ronald McDonald," Tina said.

"Well, it is," Katie said, frowning at Tina. "He's the best storyteller in the world. And he makes them all up himself. Sometimes they're real scary and sometimes sad . . . sometimes funny . . ."

"Can the twins come?" Bo asked.

"Oh, sure," I said.

The Harrises started for the back door. " 'Bye, everyone," Mrs. Harris said. "And . . . thank you all for . . . well, you know, letting Tina . . . I mean. . ." and she stopped.

"She not getting a handout," Pa said, patting Tina's shoulder. "She does a mighty fine job. We're glad to have her!"

"Come here, Tina," Mama said. "You've been watching long enough. You think you can cut the rest of the melon balls?"

On Monday's *Punchy's* was closed during the winter, spring and fall, but starting last year, Pa stayed open seven days a week in the summer. The only compromise he'd make for Ma's sake was to open for dinner only, not breakfast or lunch. Ma said it was a strange way to handle it, but she went along and at least Pa relaxed most Mondays, sleeping in the hammock, playing with Bo, swimming . . .

Ma relaxed, too, which meant she sewed all day. When Katie complained that she worked too hard, Ma said, "Listen, honey, I'm off my feet!" so Katie left her alone.

This Monday, the last week in July, Tina and I went exploring. That is, Tina explored. There was nothing for *me* to explore, I could find my way from the Land's End Motel practically to the Northport Public Library wearing a blindfold. And probably do it in fifteen minutes. But Tina decided she wanted to see some more of the town.

"Let's take Bo and then go get the twins," Tina suggested.

"Aw, no, this is one time I don't have to mind kids!" I said. "Let's go alone."

She shrugged. "Okay."

"But let's go tell the Harrises," I said.

"What *for?*" she said, sounding disgusted. "They *know* I'm over here with you."

I was about to argue with her because I kept remembering the promise I made to Mr. Harris, that I would see that he knew where Tina was all the time. But before I could say anything, Tina surprised me. "Oh, okay, S.J. We can stop down there while we're walking," she said.

"Good, okay," I said.

"Just be back in time for your shifts," Pa called as we walked off. I was barefoot, but Tina had on sneakers. She hated to walk barefoot. She said she had sensitive feet.

We stopped by the Shoreline and told Mrs. Harris we would spend the afternoon exploring Meridian. She just smiled a lot and said fine. And we walked back up to the town's main street, which was probably about a half-a-mile long. Maybe less.

"What's *that*?" Tina sneered, pointing.

"Just a store," I said. "Mrs. McBride runs it."

"*The Knit Knook*?" Tina said. "They sure get cutsie in this town. Boy!"

I smiled. I'd never thought about it before. "Yeah, guess the name's kind of silly," I said. "But what she knits isn't! Everyone thinks they're really lucky if they get one of her ski sweaters for Christmas. I got one two years ago and it still fits. It's blue and gray, with a white reindeer right up here, near the neck. She made up the whole design herself."

But Tina was already bored with the subject. "Look at that car," she said, pointing. "What the heck is it?"

"Oh, that's a '55 Chevy. It's Travis's."

"What's a Travis?"

"Travis Sumner. His father owns that gas station

and Travis has been around cars since he was born. He's rebuilding that Chevy. Isn't it nice?"

Tina wrinkled up her nose. "Might be nicer if it wasn't purple." She started to walk toward it.

"Don't," I said. "Don't fool around with it, Tina . . ."

"I won't, but the hood's up, I wanna see what it looks like inside." I watched her. She was bending over, peering into the front end of the car. When she started to walk around to get a better look at the other side, I saw her jump and quickly back away toward me.

I went over. "What is it?" I whispered.

Tina was smiling. "I interrupted a little thing in the car."

"What little thing?" I wanted to know.

"Oh, jeez, S.J., there's a couple doin' it in the back seat," she said.

"Doing what? Oh! Really?" I started to smile, too. "Who?"

"How should *I* know, for Pete's sake?" she said. "Besides, I wasn't looking at their faces!"

"Did they have their clothes off?" I asked.

Tina smirked at me. "Wouldn't you like to know? Why don't you spy on them?"

"Awww no!" I said. "Well, let's see . . . I betcha the guy is Travis because nobody would mess with his car. He'd kill anybody who touched that car. But who would the girl be? Travis never had a girlfriend in Meridian . . ."

"Why does she have to be from this town?" Tina asked.

"Well, she doesn't, but you'd figure that if she were from another town, why would he bring her back here to sit in his parked car in Sunrise Alley?" I tried to remember if Travis brought a girl to his Senior Prom last year . . .

"Let's watch 'em," Tina said, still smirking. "Come on, we'll make 'em crazy. We'll stand over there behind that store and throw little rocks at the side of the car . . ."

I grabbed her arm. "Come on, Tina, let's get away from here!"

"Don'tcha wanna know who it is in there, S.J.? Don'tcha wanna know if they have any clothes on?" She didn't move.

Just then the door of the car opened and I recognized Travis Sumner getting out from the back seat. He had *all* his clothes on. I wondered if he had heard us. Someone still in the car was struggling to get out, too—the car was a two-door—but Travis didn't turn around to help.

"Oh, God," I said, clapping my hand to my mouth. "It's Linda."

"Linda who?" Tina asked.

"Come on, while they're not looking at us," I said to Tina and we continued down the little street where buildings hid us completely from the couple in the alley.

"Linda *who*?" Tina asked again. "What's the matter?"

"Linda Merkel," I said. "Remember that day in the movies? When we first met?"

"*Earl's* Linda?"

I nodded.

"Awwww," Tina said. "That's crummy. Earl's a nice guy." I knew that Earl didn't like Tina in the beginning, especially that first night when she came into *Punchy's* with the Harrises. But after she started working, he changed his mind about her. "Hey, S.J." she said.

"What?"

"I was kidding. About their clothes . . . They had their clothes on, honest."

I looked at her.

"Really, they did!" she insisted.

"I believe you," I said. "That's not why I was looking at you . . ."

"Why then?"

I couldn't really answer her, so I just said, "You know what let's do? Let's go over to the school. The Junior High, where I'll be going. You wanna see it?"

"A school! Why would I wanna see a school!" she said.

"Don't you like school?" I asked.

"I've seen so many schools, I can't even tell 'em apart," she said. "They're all alike and they're all boring."

"How come you went to a lot of schools?" I asked, and before the question was out of my mouth, I remembered Tina'd lived with a lot of different people. I panicked for a second, but then I realized that it was a good question to ask because I wasn't supposed to know about that anyway.

Tina gave me a quick look, then sighed. "I keep changing schools because they're so *boring*. I'm trying to find one I like enough to stay there."

"Oh," was all I said.

"Okay, let's walk over to your school. Is there a playground?" she said.

"Sure. The elementary school's across the field. I'll race you."

"Thanks a lot, I don't know where it is," she said.

"Follow me!" I broke into a run and when she spotted the school 'way at the end of the main street of the town, she sprinted ahead of me and outran me by a mile!

She was already on one of the swings when I came panting up to her. I flopped down on the swing next to hers.

"You're fast!" I gasped.

"You have to be, in the city," she said and laughed, too. "Hey, there's a merry-go-round! Come on, I'll push you!" She jumped up and ran over to it. I followed and leaped on, while she was struggling to get it going. When it got some momentum, she jumped on, too, and we went around a few times until I got nauseated and got off. Then we lay in the grass next to it.

"We don't have grass playgrounds in the city," Tina said, looking up at the sky. "Maybe I'll go to this school."

"You can't," I said, "You'll be going back to the city after the summer." She didn't say anything.

"Won't you?" I said. She still didn't answer. "Those cabins aren't heated or anything in the winter. Nobody could live there . . ."

"Who needs heat!" Tina said. "They didn't have heat, the Pilgrims . . ."

I laughed out loud. "I can just see you as a Pilgrim," I said, and she giggled. "Those cute little black dresses and aprons . . ."

"And those white hats!" she cackled. "Oh, yeah! I'd be a great Pilgrim! I'd show 'em how to make cutoffs out of those black dresses . . ."

". . . and halter tops out of the aprons!" It made us really giggly and we slapped at the ground and each other. "Anyway," I said finally, "they did have fireplaces and big ovens. The Shoreline just has a little electric heater."

". . . a little electric heater . . ." Tina said thoughtfully. "Pretty deserted in the winter, huh?"

"Yeah . . . why?"

She grinned. "Oh, I was just thinking that it sounds better than the back seat of a car. You know, for Travis and what's-her-name . . ."

"Linda," I said. "She's always been Earl's girlfriend. Why do you suppose she's with *Travis*? That was weird."

"Georgia used to say 'When the cat's away the mouse will play,' " Tina said.

"Who's Georgia?" I asked.

"Oh, just . . . someone I stayed with once. Anyway, it means, when the cat's working in the restaurant, the mouse will neck in a purple car."

"You mean because Earl hasn't had time to go out she just up and found somebody else?" I asked.

"Wouldn't be the first time it happened," Tina said. "Now. Do we tell Earl, or what?"

"Tell *Earl*?" I hadn't even thought of it.

"Yeah! Don't you think he should know?" she asked.

I shook my head. "Not from me," I said. "Are you kidding?"

"No, I think he should know he's being cheated on. I hate people who cheat!" She sat up quickly.

"Hey . . . look," I said. "Don't say anything yet. Let's think about it awhile, okay? Maybe they broke up already or something."

"They didn't. I know. Earl was talking about her yesterday."

"Well, look, let's wait and see what happens. Please, Tina?" I hated to tattle. And it wasn't our business anyway. "Maybe Earl will find out on his own."

"I hate cheaters," she repeated. "Come on, let's

go back. It's almost time for work." She looked at her watch.

"I never saw that watch before," I said. "Where did you get it?"

She quickly drew back her hand. "I—I don't wear it much. Who needs a watch? I've just been wearing it a while now so I can tell when it's time for work. I don't wanna be late, you know?"

"So where'd you get the watch? It's nice."

She looked at it like she was seeing it for the first time. "Yeah. Guess so. It . . . It was a present. My mother sent it from . . . somewhere."

"Oh. Nice present," I said. "It's fancy."

Tina looked at me for a long time. I looked right back until I just got too uncomfortable, so I looked away. It was such a funny stare she was giving me.

Finally she said, "Hey, uh, Sarajane?"

"Yeah?"

She looked down at the watch and then back at me. Couple of times. Then she said, "Nothing. We gotta go," and got up and ran down the playground hill.

Chapter Nine

When Tina and I got to the restaurant, the first one we saw was Earl Peterson. He was unfolding a white tablecloth and spreading it over table two, and he was whistling.

My face got all red. I could tell because it was burning me.

I grabbed Tina's sleeve and stepped back.

Tina turned around. "What'sa matter with *you?* Hey, your face is all red."

"I . . . feel funny. Don't you?" I jerked my head toward Earl, whose back was to us.

"No, I don't feel funny," Tina said. "I feel mad. I still wanna tell him . . ."

"Shh!" I said quickly. "It's none of our business. Don't tell him. Besides, look, he's whistling and everything . . ."

"You know what, S.J.?" Tina said. "You're acting like *you're* the one who did something wrong to him. It's not *your* fault."

"Don't say anything, Tina, don't! Please!" I begged.

She sighed. "Okay, okay. I won't say anything. For now. But don't *you* walk around like you lost your last friend, either, every time you go near him. And you better get that red out of your face."

"How?"

"Murine. Gets the red out," she said and we both laughed.

"What's black and white and red all over?" I asked her, giggling.

"What?" she said.

"A Pilgrim before using Murine!" We got hysterical and almost knocked over a chair.

"Be careful!" Earl yelled. "Boy, you do that when the people start coming in, we're in trouble. Come on, Sarajane, your ma wants you to fix the hamburger patties for the kids' portions. Tina, you do the melon balls."

Four families came in at once at six o'clock, and they kept coming. It was a big night. Tina bused for Scotty and Charley Harmon bused for Earl. Charley worked part-time in the summer. Tina did as good a job as Charley, and he was a boy and two years older!

"Sara!" Ma called as I was going through the "out" door into the dining room. "Check to see that we've got all the fruitcup dishes in here . . . I want to get them washed so we'll have them for sherbet!"

"Right," I said and went out. I spotted Mr. Hopper sitting alone at table five. He was reading a menu, and I went over to him.

"The meatloaf won't be ready for a while," I said, "but we've got some terrific-looking steak."

"Hi, there, Sarajane," he said. "I'm really not too hungry. Would it be too boring if I just had a salad?"

I wrinkled my nose at him. He said such funny things. "I guess it'd be okay," I told him. "Uh, Bo's been asking about . . . you know . . . when you're gonna, uh," I shrugged and smiled.

"Oh," he said. "Hold a soiree?"

"What's a swah-ray?"

"Have a story night, right?"

"Yeah," I answered, embarrassed.

"How about this very night?" he said with a nod.

"This very night would be terrific!" I cried. "Oh . . . but . . ." I looked around.

"I know, I know, working girl. Don't worry, we'll do it after you're through. After the rush. How's that?"

"Let me go check!" I raced back into the kitchen. "Ma, Pa! Mr. Hopper's telling stories tonight. Can we all go? It'll be after the rush. What time do you think that'll be?"

"Tonight? Tonight?" Bo was ready to leave right then.

"Oh, good!" Katie cried from her place at the stove. "Can we go, Ma?"

"Sure," Ma answered. "Scotty, there's something the matter with this oven. The meatloaf should've been done fifteen minutes ago. See if you can push the fish and the steaks for now."

"Okay, Miz Punch," Scotty said.

"I'll stick around and help you," Tina said. "I'm not goin' to any Kindergarten story hour."

"You go, Tina," Ma said. "You won't be sorry. Pick up the twins and take them, too."

"No way," Tina said.

"Hey, Tina," I said, going over to her. "Look, I promise you, it's not baby stuff. Please go. The twins would like it, too. Come on, okay?"

She sighed. "Oh, boy," she said. But I knew it meant she would go.

"Sarajane," Mom said, "Do I have all the fruitcup dishes or not?"

"Oh, wow!" I said and went back into the dining room. I picked up four dishes and told Mr. Hopper it was all set.

When our group got to Kozy, a bunch of kids was already there. Some of the Harmons, and Neddy Sumner, Rosemarie and Sylvia Rice, Carrie Raymond . . . a few others. And there were some summer kids I didn't know.

Mr. Hopper was sitting in a rocking chair next to the door of his cabin. The kids were sitting all over his porch and the cabin railing. It was just about dark, so Mr. Hopper put on the little light on the ceiling of the porch. It was a yellow bug light and I watched all the gnats and moths and mosquitos fly up and buzz around it.

When we were all quiet, Mr. Hopper passed around a big bowl of popcorn and started talking. The first story he told was really funny. It was about this little five-year-old kid who got a bill from a big fancy store in New York for a lounge chair with built-in stereo headphones. The kid tried to convince the store that he never bought the chair and that he didn't even have a credit card, he was only five, but all he ever reached were computers. And the computers kept sending him more bills, with interest adding up, and letters that said he was unco-operative. Finally, the store sent people to take the chair back and they were very upset when the kid didn't have it. So they took his rocker, with the decals of Batman and Robin on it. But it turned out all right because the kid ended up with cards from the Diners Club, American Express and Master Charge.

Tina laughed her head off at that story and I did, too, but I think I laughed more from watching Tina laugh than from the story. Bo said he didn't think it was funny that the men took away the kid's rocker.

The second story seemed kind of a sad one. Mr. Hopper's voice got real quiet and dreamy and I began to get a little sleepy. I tried to stay awake and listen but my mind began to wander.

I looked at Tina. She was sitting on the railing, leaning against a post. Each of her feet was resting on the shoulder of a Samios twin on the floor. Georgie and Teddy looked more exactly alike in the glow of the bug light than they ever looked before. Listening to Mr. Hopper, they both had their mouths open and their eyes half-closed. Since one of them wasn't talking, I couldn't tell them apart at all. I tried to remember if I had ever heard Teddy say *anything* and decided I didn't think I had.

Bo had his head in Katie's lap and she was patting his hair, twirling it every now and then with her finger. They were all listening so hard. His voice was so . . . nice. That's what I remember thinking last, and then I fell asleep.

". . . in a *trance* or something?" somebody was saying. I looked up. It was Tina, standing over me, yelling. I shook my head. The only kids left on Mr. Hopper's porch were Bo and Katie and Tina and the twins. Bo was asleep in Katie's lap. One of the twins was sitting on Mr. Hopper's knee and the other was on the floor, leaning against his leg.

"I *said*, are you in a trance or something," Tina repeated. "I been talkin' to a wall for five minutes!"

"Hey, I'm sorry," I said. I felt terrible. Mr. Hopper must have thought I was really rude. "I fell asleep . . . I tried not to." I looked past Tina at a woman coming up the porch steps. "Tina? It's so late . . ." It was Mrs. Samios. "I thought . . . you bring the boys home by now." She had a little accent I hadn't noticed before.

"Oh, uh, the stories just ended, Mrs. Samios," Tina said. "I'm sorry."

"No, *I'm* sorry," Mr. Hopper said, getting up, holding the twin. "I shouldn't have rambled on so long."

Mrs. Samios reached for whatever twin was in Mr. Hopper's arms. "I take them home now. Thank you, thank you . . ." She put him down gently and took each twin by a hand, walking them toward the Shoreline.

"Mr. Hopper, I'm sorry I fell asleep," I said, as I stood up. "I really didn't want to . . . The story about the little boy in the Botanical Gardens . . . it sounded so good."

"Oh, Sarajane, that's all right," he said and patted my shoulder. "You had a big day. Anyway, sometimes even *I* fall asleep over my stories." He laughed, or coughed or something, and went into his cabin, with a little wave at the other kids.

Tina called after him, "Hey, thanks!"

"Let's go," I said to Katie, but she didn't move. I shook her and she got Bo up on his feet and then herself. We all stumbled our way to Tina's cabin, except for Tina, who seemed pretty wide awake.

"Okay," she said to me. "Okay." She nodded her head up and down.

"Okay, what?"

"Okay, you were right. The guy was good, the

stories were good. I'm glad ya told me about it." She looked very serious.

"Oh, well, yeah . . ." I said, "Me, too, Only I really *am* sorry I missed the second story. What was it about? I remember there was this boy, about seven years old . . ."

"Nine," Tina said.

"Okay, nine, and he lived in Brooklyn with his mean aunt . . ."

"She wasn't mean, she just didn't give a damn," Tina said.

"Oh. Okay, so he ran away to live in the Brooklyn Botanical Gardens all by himself with the plants."

"Right," Tina said. "And the plants became his friends and they all had names and different personalities and it was warm there . . . and nice."

"And what happened?" I wanted to know.

"Well, the kid was making it, see, but one day this old lady caught on to him. She found out he never went home or anything, and she told on him and he got sent back. To his aunt."

"Is that the end?"

"Yeah. There's always some old lady around to louse things up. Kids could make it fine on their own if people would just let 'em alone." We were at her cabin.

I looked at Bo, holding Katie's hand. "You really think they could, Tina?" I asked.

Tina made a disgusted face and waved her hand.

"Who knows?" she said. "See ya tomorrow.

But we didn't. She didn't show up all morning and neither did the twins. When everybody went down for the lunch shift, I took Bo to the beach. We went to Tina's cabin right away but nobody was there. I wondered if she had gone to New York to see her "worker," or whatever they called it, but I didn't think so, because the last time she went, she made up a big story about going to the city and I figured she'd do the same if she went again. This was Tuesday, and not Tina's regular work day, so I couldn't count on seeing her at the restaurant, either, unless she just showed up anyway, which she sometimes did.

Bo ran ahead of me right into the water. I was just about to yell at him, when I heard him call to a sun-bathing body on a blanket. "Hi, Miz Harris!" he hollered as he went by.

Mrs. Harris. I ran over to the blanket, remembering to keep an eye on Bo. I thought of the firecrackers every time that kid got away from me!

"Mrs. Harris?"

She opened her eyes and squinted at me. Then she sat up and put on a pair of sunglasses. "Oh, hi, Sarajane. Was that Bo who just said hello?"

"Yes . . ." I said. I was just about to ask her where the heck Tina was, when Georgie ran into me and knocked me down on Mrs. Harris's blanket.

"Oh, Georgie, don't *run* like that!" his mother called after him. "So sorry, Sarajane," she said. She had Teddy by the hand. "Mrs. Harris . . . We were looking for Tina. I was hoping that she could be with the twins while I shop for a while . . . You think . . .?"

Mrs. Harris smiled up at her. "Oh, I'm sorry, Mrs. Samios. Tina's in New York today, visiting her mother." And she began to oil herself with suntan lotion.

My mouth dropped open, but she didn't look at me. She went on oiling herself. I didn't even see Mrs. Samios walk away.

"Her *mother*?" I said.

"Yah, we got a call from Mr. Gerardi early this morning. Her mother wanted to see her, so Jim, Mr. Harris, took her in with him when he went on his shift. He's got the eight to four again . . ."

"Mr. Gerardi?" I asked.

"Her case worker. You know." She put down the tube of lotion and looked at me. "You *don't* know," she said.

"Oh, I know, I know," I said quickly, "I just didn't know his name." I suddenly remembered Bo and checked him. He was fine; he was a good swimmer.

"Is Tina's mother back from Europe?" I asked.

"Europe!" Mrs. Harris said, frowning. "She wasn't in—Did Tina tell you her mother was in Europe?"

I looked down at my lap. "Yes, ma'am. Please don't tell her I told you."

She smiled and put her hand on mine. "Please don't tell her I told *you*," she said. "Tina's mother is—*lives*—in New York City, but Tina doesn't see her very often. This morning . . . well, it was kind of a surprise call. She just wanted to know if she could see Tina

.117.

today and it happened to work out all right, because of Jim's day shift. Look, Sarajane . . ." she wiggled around on the blanket. "Tina doesn't always, well— she doesn't always tell the truth about everything, but . . . but she really likes you. She really does. It hasn't always been easy, for Tina. So . . . don't hold it against her, okay?"

"Oh, no," I said. "No, I don't hold it against her."

"We like Tina a lot," she went on. "We'd like to keep her . . . We'd like to give her a little better than what she's had, you know? We never had a daughter. We've got two married sons, one lives in Omaha and the other in West Virginia, so you might guess we don't get to see them very much. Jim loves kids, he works with a youth group in the city, and he sees lots of foster kids getting a raw deal. Foster parents, too, you'd be surprised. So we wanted to make a real family for Tina, and for ourselves, too."

I stood up to check Bo, but sat right down again so she'd know I wasn't leaving or anything. But she didn't seem to notice.

"That's one of the reasons we came up here for the summer. It's a rough commute for Jim, 'specially when he's on the midnight-to-eight shift, but we knew she never had a vacation like this before . . ."

"Mrs. Harris?"

"Yes, honey?"

"Um, remember last time, you wanted me to sleep over after Tina was in New York? Because of the nightmares?" I decided that with Mrs. Harris, I'd just forget about who knew what and who told who what and who had which secrets.

"I remember," she said.

"Well, do you think she might have them again tonight? Would you want me to sleep over again?" I asked. I never invited myself anywhere before. Mama would probably have a fit. But this was different.

Mrs. Harris looked like she might cry. "Oh, honey . . . That's very nice. I'm not sure how today will be for Tina. I just don't know, I don't know what her mother wants. I think we'd better forget it tonight— I'm not sure what mood she'll be in. But I would like you to sleep over again sometime soon. Okay?"

"Okay," I said, and wondered what story Tina would tell me about the day.

She showed up at the restaurant at about eight that night. It wasn't a busy night and the rush was over. I was out front busing, and she came in through the kitchen, so I didn't see her until I walked back in there. She was tying on her apron.

"Hi," she said, like nothing happened. "I'll bus, you do the dishes."

I started to say "Okay" and do it, but I just couldn't stand it, so I said right out, "Where were you today?"

"New York," she said, adjusting the apron straps.

"Have a good time?" I asked, peering at her face, which she wouldn't let me see.

"It was okay," she said, and walked into the dining room.

By nine o'clock, there wasn't a customer left in the restaurant. That wasn't too unusual, but it was about the slowest we'd been all month. Everything was practically cleared up and we were getting ready to go, when Linda Merkel came in. I didn't know who it was because I was helping Ma unload the dishwasher, but Pa heard the footsteps out front and told Earl to tell whoever it was the kitchen was closed. He went out and didn't come back, so Tina went to investigate. In a minute she came stomping back into the kitchen.

"Guess who it is out there," she said to me.

"A Pilgrim convention," I said.

"Wrong. It's Linda."

"Is she with Travis?"

"Linda and Travis out front?" Katie asked, rattling plates.

"No," Tina said. "Just Linda."

"For God's sake, whisper, will you?" I said. "The whole world doesn't have to know."

"Okay, okay. She's alone, talking to Earl," Tina whispered.

"Oh, good. Maybe she's telling him herself that she fell in love with Travis," I said. "That'll be hard but at least it's better than him not knowing."

"Not her," Tina said. "I bet she's conning him. She wouldn't tell him she's got another guy. Why should she, when she can have two? Maybe more."

Tina and I looked at each other. From the looks of the kitchen, we still had maybe five minutes more before Pa would turn out the lights and head for home. Neither of us said anything, but we both made a beeline for the exit door leading to the dining room.

I stopped suddenly before going out and Tina ran into me.

"Ow! What th—"

"We can't just go out there," I said. "We have to look like we're doing something. Everything's cleaned up out there, there's nothing to do."

"Oh," she said. "Hey! How 'bout if we set the tables for breakfast? That'll be something to do. C'mon, let's get clean dishes." She headed for the shelf.

"Wait a minute," I said, nudging her. "Pa? Want us to set up for breakfast before we go?"

"Breakfast? No, honey, we don't do that. I don't like the silver to be out all night on the tables . . ."

"What's the difference?" I said.

"Oh. All right," Pa said and flopped down on the kitchen stool. "Hurry up, though, I want to get home, honey."

"I'll take the kids, Mike," Ma said and went out the kitchen door with Bo and Katie.

Tina and I walked into the dining room armed with tablecloths, silver and napkins.

Out of the corner of my eye, I saw Earl in the far corner, opposite the front door. I couldn't see Linda, because she was leaning against the wall and Earl was in front of her, with his arm resting against the wall over her head.

"Let's set up Station Five," Tina said to me. Station

Five was the group of tables right next to Linda and Earl's wall.

"Good idea," I said, and we walked over. We didn't look directly at them but kept sneaking looks out of the corners of our eyes. Tina and I kept jockeying for the best position. Both of us wanted to set the place that was facing them without having to keep turning around. Finally, Tina motioned to me with one finger and we moved over into Station Three.

"Didn't I tell you?" she whispered. "They're not breaking up. They're kissing!"

"That's why I couldn't hear any conversation!" I said.

"That's why, dummy," Tina said and poked me, laughing. Then she was serious. "I don't care who she messes around with, but I don't like her messing around behind somebody's back. Somebody that she's supposed to like, that's the thing. That's what I can't stand. When you have a friend, you have a friend for life!"

I smiled at her and stuck out my hand. She didn't smile back but took my hand and shook it. Up and down. Hard.

Chapter Ten

"Hey, S.J., did you know Mr. Hopper likes to fish?" Tina asked me late one morning after Ma had gone to the restaurant for the lunch shift. I was deciding whether or not to take Bo swimming. It looked like it might rain.

"Sure, I know. He loves to fish. I went with him once last summer.

"Well, he's going out around now and he asked me if we could go with him."

"We? You mean you and me?" I asked.

"Yeah, you and me. Who'd you think?"

"And what am I supposed to do with Bo?" I said. "Besides, look, it's probably gonna rain."

"It's not gonna rain," Tina said. "We could leave Bo with Mrs. Samios. Jeez, I'm always taking care of *them*, and so are you. So just this once they can watch Bo for us."

"Well . . ."

"When else can we go?" she nagged. "I'm not working lunch today, but I do most every other day. And you work dinners, and so do I . . ."

"Well, sometimes he fishes at dawn . . . That's really the best time, you know," I said.

"Dawn! You gotta be kidding," Tina said.

"Oh, all right. But only if it's okay with Mrs. Samios," I told her.

It was okay. Mrs. Samios said she'd be real glad to have Bo, and the three kids were happy about the arrangement. Tina and I walked down to where Karefree kept its row boats and found Mr. Hopper putting a tackle box and some rods into the Kozy Kabin boat. He was wearing khaki shorts and a sport shirt that was buttoned wrong.

He waved his arm over his head. "Hi, hi," he said. "We're goin' fishin'. Go-in' fishin'!"

I looked at him. "You all right, Mr. Hopper?" I asked.

"Of course, of course, my little dear," he said. "Did —you—know . . . that there is a Northeast wind today? Did you know that?"

I bit my lip, "A Northeast wind? That means . . . fishing shouldn't be too good . . ."

"*Give* that little girl a dollar. And look at the lake. Look, look," he said. He sounded so strange.

I looked at the lake. It was choppy. There were some white caps on it.

"It's choppy," I said.

"And you know what else?" he asked, grinning. "*Prob*-ably, it's going to storm. Prob . . ."

Tina said, "So? Does that mean we're not going?"

"NO!" Mr. Hopper cried. "Of course not! *We* are going fishing! Right now. Uh oh—I only have two rods. Two rods. You girls mind sharing a rod? Or I could share a rod or we all could share . . ."

"It's okay," Tina said. She couldn't wait to get out in the boat. I could wait. Mr. Hopper was acting weird. I thought maybe he was sick.

"Well, what are you waiting for!" Mr. Hopper yelled, waving his two fishing rods. "In, in! Get in! Lad-ies first, then the gent. That's me, the gent!"

I gave Tina a look, but she was jumping in the boat. "Listen, Mr. Hopper, uh, why don't I row?" I suggested. I was thinking that Mr. Hopper wasn't exactly himself, and if there was any thunder, I wanted to be able to row us right back, quick. I also didn't want to go out too far.

"My dear girl!" he said, sounding insulted. "Don't you think I am able to propel a simple rowboat around a simple lake? I—" He slipped and fell into the boat, banging his knee.

"Oh, hey—" Tina said and moved to help him, but he pulled away. "I'm per-fect-ly all right, my dear," he said, but his knee was bleeding. It must've scraped when he fell. He didn't seem to notice though, and I just moved into the seat in the middle, slipped the oars into the oarlocks and began to row. Mr. Hopper kept mumbling "per-fect-ly all right . . . per-fect-ly . . ."

The only one who fished was Tina. And she didn't know how. I tried to show her, but it was hard because I had to keep holding onto the oars. The lake *was* choppy and I could have lost an oar if I wasn't careful, so I just had to talk to Tina about what to do and that wasn't easy. At least she was using artificial bait, so we didn't have to worry about real worms. Mr. Hopper just sat there. He had stopped mumbling and was just staring out at the water, letting me move us slowly around. I kept an eye on the sky and an eye on Tina. There were no eyes left for Mr. Hopper and for once I was glad he was quiet. I didn't know what was wrong with him. He did have kind of funny moods, but nothing like this before. Lots of times I didn't understand the words he used, but I always felt like I wasn't supposed to anyway, like it was his private joke. His own private joke, and he was letting me look at just a little of it, and not making fun of me or anything like that. But now . . . I just couldn't figure it out.

"*Tina!*" I hollered. "Quit it! You're reeling backwards! You're gonna screw up your line . . ." I sighed. "Forget it, it's too late." Her line was wrapped outside the reel, inside the reel, around the reel.

"Awwww," she said, looking down at the mess. "What do I do now?"

"Nothing," I said. "Put the rod down, I'm rowing back."

"Come on, S.J. . . ." she begged.

"Look, Tina, I can't fix the line and I can't show you what to do because I have to hang onto these oars. And he's . . ." I looked toward Mr. Hopper, who had gone to sleep on the bottom of the boat ". . . no help. What the heck's wrong with him? You think he just hasn't had enough sleep? He's really tired."

Tina threw back her head and laughed. "S.J., you dodo . . . You really don't know what's the matter with him?" I just stared at her. "Man!" she cried. "You teach me how to fish, I'll teach you about the world!" and she roared again. We had reached the shore. I took off my sandals and held them while I waded in. Everyone had to get out of the boat before I could pull it up on land.

"Come on," Tina said. "You take his fishing stuff and I'll take him. Let's go, Mr. Hopper. Laa-st stop. End of the line. Beddy-bye time," she sang, as she pulled him by his arm.

"Maybe he's sick," I said. "Should I get someone?"

"You may have to if I can't get him on his feet,"

Tina said. "He's drunk as a skunk!" She laughed again, to herself this time. "Just like good ol' Uncle Marty!"

"He's *drunk?*" I asked. "*Really?* Is *that* what's wrong?"

"Couldn't you tell?" Tina asked. "Haven't you ever seen a drunk before? Man, you work in a restaurant; *Punchy's* serves wine and beer. Hasn't anyone ever got zonked in there?"

I thought about it and shook my head. I remember that Pa had bought a wine-and-beer license a couple of years ago because he talked about it at that time, but not only couldn't I remember anyone getting drunk, I didn't even remember wine or beer being served, even though it must have been. Pa and Ma didn't drink anything except on holidays, and that was before dinner. This was eleven-thirty in the morning!

Tina was struggling with Mr. Hopper. She had his left arm over her shoulders and she was propping him up with her right arm and her right side. "See if you can manage that stuff with one hand, S.J.," she said, "and get on the other side of him. Come on. Kozy isn't that far, we can manage it."

"Okay," I said, "but let me pull the boat up first."

Somehow we got him home, up his porch steps and onto his bed. Tina unbuttoned his shirt and wiped his face with a damp washcloth. We put his fishing tackle against a wall. Then we went outside and collapsed on his porch.

"Man, he weighs more than you'd think," Tina said, panting, "I'm beat!"

"Why would he do that?" I wanted to know. "Why would he get drunk like that! He doesn't look like the kind that would do that."

Tina dropped her hands in her lap with a thud and looked at me. Her mouth dropped open. "S.J. . . ." she said.

"What?"

"Nothin'."

"No, what? What were you going to say?"

"You've known this guy for almost two summers now, right?"

"Yeah . . ."

"And I hardly know him at all, right?"

"Yeah . . ."

"Well, I know him better than you."

"What do you mean?"

Tina licked her lips. "I knew him right away from that night he told the stories. That poor guy . . . Remember the story about the little kid who ran away to live with the plants?" I nodded. "Well . . . that little kid . . . the way Hopper talked about him . . . You could just tell he knew exactly how that kid felt. There he was, living with some crabby aunt who didn't give two hoots in hell about him—preachin' at him about how the devil was gonna get him any second now—there he was, and he just decided to split, baby, I mean he just took off and smelled the flowers! Until that old witch caught him after the place was closed. Hopper really wanted that kid to make it, but he knew he couldn't. He couldn't because . . . because it's hard to make it alone. And it hurts to be lonely . . ."

I could feel my heart thumping. Tina's voice . . . as she was talking to me . . . her voice got softer, deeper. It was the other voice she used when she had the chain-thing.

". . . he's such a lonely guy," she was saying, "There's something he wants so bad . . ." she shook her head. "I don't know what it is, I don't know. But you can see the wanting and you can hear it . . ." She stuck out her jaw suddenly. And when she spoke again, the other voice was gone. "He's a lonely sucker, just a poor sap, that's what he is. He doesn't belong to nobody, nobody gives a damn, so what if he boozes at eleven-thirty in the morning? Who cares? And you know who you sound like? You sound like the aunt in the story, preachin' that the devil's gonna get him instead of thinkin' about what's inside of him!"

Oh, God. That was true, I never thought about it. I just never thought. I started to cry. Just like a stupid baby. And that's when the other voice came back again out of Tina's mouth.

"Hey, don't cry. Don't cry, S.J. How could you know, anyway? Hey, it's okay, it's okay," she said over and over, and I stopped.

She was late that evening for the dinner shift.
Katie said, "Where's Tina? She's usually early."

"*You're* asking about Tina?" I said. "You change your mind about her, Katherine Ann Punch?"

"I dunno . . ." Katie said, biting her lower lip. "She's changed since she's been here. Sometimes she doesn't seem so mean any more."

"You can't tell people by the way they act all the time," I said.

"Well, smarty," she said, putting her hand on her hip, "how are you supposed to tell them then?"

"You just . . . you just have to . . ." I couldn't find the words. "You have to keep remembering that they may be different inside than the way they act, that's all."

Chapter Eleven

Friday was one of the days Tina worked lunches
and I stayed home with the kids, which I usually did
at lunch time anyway. Mrs. Harris knew that, I guess,
because that's the time she picked to come over to see
me. Bo and I were eating lunch in the kitchen when
I looked up and saw her at the screen door.

"Can I come in, Sarajane?" she asked and I realized I hadn't said or done anything, just sat there
looking at her.

"Sure. Oh, sure. Sorry." I got up, but she somehow
got through the job of opening the screen door and

coming in without my help. "Bo, you finished?" I asked.

"Yup."

"Well, get in your bathing suit, we'll go to the lake," I told him. He was off like a shot. He never got tired of swimming. Pa said he figured him for the Olympics some day.

"Is Tina okay, Mrs. Harris?" I asked.

"Yah, she's fine, but . . . um, Mr. Gerardi's coming up here this afternoon . . . He wants to talk to Tina about . . . her mother and see how she's living up here and what it's like for her, you know?"

I really didn't know, so I didn't say anything.

"Did Tina tell you about that visit with her mother last Tuesday?" Mrs. Harris asked.

I coughed. "No, ma'am."

"Well, she didn't tell us, either, but Mr. Gerardi did. He goes with her, you see, whenever she sees Mrs. Gogolav— I still can't pronounce that name . . . Anyway, he's a nice man, Mr. Gerardi. He doesn't have to come up here, doesn't have to do that at all. But he cares about Tina, he's important in her life. He's been with her through, well, through all the homes she's been in and everything . . ."

I wanted to ask Mrs. Harris about those homes but I just couldn't. There was something about the way she talked to me when she was telling about Tina. It was as if she wasn't really talking to me at all, but to herself, or someone far away. She never looked at me at all when she got going about Tina . . .

.133.

". . . and he told me on the phone just now that Tina's mother's thinking of taking her back. After all these years . . ."

"Taking her back!" I cried. "You mean to the city? Away from you? Away from *here*?" But this is the best place of all . . .

"He said 'just *thinking*,' Sarajane, so I don't know. Anyway, I'm on my way to the restaurant to tell Tina he'll be up for an hour or so this afternoon and so now I *would* like to take you up on your offer to sleep over tonight, if that's okay with you. I'll talk to your mother down at *Punchy's* . . ."

"It's fine with me," I said, "but let her come over here tonight, instead of me going there. Just . . . for the change. Tell my mama I asked that. I'm sure it'll be okay."

She thanked me and left.

"Hey, are we going to the lake or not!" Bo yelled from the yard.

I almost said "NOT!" but I didn't. After all, it wasn't *his* fault.

I got to meet Mr. Gerardi. He and Tina walked down to the lake together about four-thirty, and Bo and I were still there. I should have been home by that time but I just hadn't gone.

"Hey, S.J.!" she said. I looked up at Mr. Gerardi. He was a short guy. Bald, with a moustache. Thin. He was sweating a lot. "This's Paulo. Friend of mine. From New York."

He put out his hand and grinned at me. "Hi, S.J.," he said. "Tina's talked a lot about you." Tina shot him a dirty look. "I'm glad to know you."

I couldn't say, "Tina hasn't even mentioned you," so I just shook his hand.

"I didn't know you'd still be here . . ." Tina said.

"Yeah, well, I'm leaving," I said, waving Bo in. "I hafta be home, you know . . . Uh, I saw Mrs. Harris before, and I got this idea, um, on the spur of the moment, that maybe you could sleep over at my house tonight."

"Oh. Okay. Did she say it was okay?" Tina asked. Mr. Gerardi gave Tina a quick look.

I nodded. "I haven't asked Ma yet, but I'm sure it'll be all right."

"Okay, see ya down there," she said, meaning the dinner shift.

Mr. Gerardi moved her further down the shore, while I got our towels and stuff together. He was a city man. He didn't know how water carries sound and I could hear every word he was saying, even though he was 'way down the beach.

". . . my little Tina asking permission, just like a regular kid? I couldn't believe my ears," he was saying. Tina laughed. "Sleeping at a friend's house, just like a regular kid? I don't believe it. Not my little scrapper. What happened to that little terror we all know and love who throws dishes at her foster mother?"

Nothing from Tina. I folded and re-folded Bo's towel four times.

"Should I tell S.J. to hide her valuables when Tina Gogo comes into her house?"

"Get-out-of-here!" Tina said.

"Ah, little Tina. Tina the Terror," he said. "You finally making it? After all this time? Did what I said to you sink in? Or is it this place? And that girl . . ."

Tina didn't answer.

"Did you tell her about you?" he asked.

Tina turned away from him and walked on down the beach. He followed her and then I couldn't hear any more. "Come on, Bo, get it moving, for Pete's sake!" I yelled and we walked up to the road.

When the dinner shift ended that night and Pa and Ma had locked the main entrance, I looked around for Tina's bag, but didn't see it.

"Where's your stuff?" I asked her. "For overnight."

"What stuff?" she said, hanging up her apron. "I thought you were kidding."

"You thought I was *kidding*! You mean you're not sleeping over tonight?" I was really upset. "I don't kid when I invite people," I said, "and I think—"

But she was laughing. "Hey, hey, take it easy!" She opened a cabinet door and took out a shopping bag. "See?" she said, holding it up. "I was just putting you on . . . I got my stuff . . . See?"

I didn't say anything.

"I just wanted to make sure it was really okay. For

me to spend the night. Just making sure, that's all."
She started for the door. "Well?" she said, turning
back to me. "What are you standing there for?"

We slept on the sun porch. It used to have just
screen windows all around it, but since the heating oil
went up so high, Pa had storm windows built for it
for the winter. It was nice, because not only did we
save the money on heat, but now we had an extra
room in the cold months. That was where we had our
Christmas tree last year.

Now, of course, the screens were back up. It was a
good place. Everyone else was sleeping upstairs. I
thought, whatever Tina does or says when the lights
are out, no one will hear.

I wouldn't look inside her shopping bag, but I
couldn't help wondering if she had brought her chain-
thing. And a lot of other thoughts went through my
head. First, I figured I'd make a show of being real
tired and wanting to sleep, so Tina would feel free to
say what she wanted to. But then I thought, wow that's
awful! I would be listening in on her, just like a cheat
—the thing she hates most. Making believe I was asleep
so she would say her secret things.

I felt sick. I wanted so bad to hear Tina talk to the
chain-thing, but I didn't want to cheat. I tried to think
that if I did listen in on purpose that it was for Tina's
own good. The more I could help, the better friend
I could be. But that wasn't really true, because you can

be a friend without knowing everything about somebody, especially her secrets. So I decided that what I
would do would be not to stay awake on purpose, like
I had planned. What I would do was, if I was awake,
then okay, it wouldn't be my fault. And if I fell asleep,
then I fell asleep.

When the light was out, I thought, maybe I could
get Tina to talk to *me* instead of the chain-thing. Then
it would be out in the open. I would get her to talk
and it wouldn't be cheating.

"Hey, Tina? That friend of yours, Mr. Gerardi?" I
began.

"Did I tell you his last name?" she asked.

Oh, God. She hadn't. She said Paulo, or something
like that. Oh, my God. Now I'd have to lie, I'd have
to. I am so stupid sometimes . . .

"Well, sure, how else would I know it?" I said.

"I dunno. How would you? I don't call him that,
though, I call him Paulo. Anyway, what about him?"

I held onto the side of my cot.

"I said, what about him?" she repeated.

I tried to make my voice not shake with my body.

"He's nice. It was nice of him to come all the way up
here to see you."

"He's okay," she said.

"How come he didn't stay over?" I was still so upset I wasn't saying any of the things I wanted to say.

"Stay over! Why would he do that?" she asked.

"I don't know," I said.

"You know what let's do Monday?" Tina asked.

"Let's be spies and follow that Linda around and see where she goes." She sounded sleepy.

All right, just as well. I'll go to sleep, too.

But I couldn't fall asleep. I was still upset over my slip about Mr. Gerardi. Tina must really be tired or she would have caught it, I just know it. Oh, please, I prayed, don't let her remember in the morning. If she ever thought I was a cheat . . .

But it wasn't my fault I knew what I knew. People told me, I didn't snoop. Wasn't my fault. I had almost decided that it *really* wasn't my fault when I heard a little clink. My eyes flew open.

Tina had pulled the chain out from under her blankets. I could see it easily in the moonlight. I figured she must have stuck it inside her bed while I was washing up. She was looking at it, not at me, and before she had a chance to wrap her hand around the thing on the end. I saw what it was . . . It was a locket. And it was in the shape of a heart, just like the old-fashioned ones Ma always admires at tag sales but never buys.

A great big gold heart. If Tina ever wore it for real it'd probably weigh her down.

"Hi, you know where we are, we're at S.J.'s house," she whispered to the heart. She was lying on her stomach with her lips real close to the locket, while the chain hung limply to the pillow.

"Yes, I know," the other voice answered. The other voice was supposed to be the locket talking, I knew. But why the locket? "That's nice," the other voice continued. "It's nice to have a friend, isn't it?" I closed my eyes.

"Yeah. He says I may be going back there," she said.

"I know," the other voice replied.

"I don't think I'm going to go, okay?"

"It's all right . . ." the other voice answered.

"He hasn't told me anything for sure yet," Tina said. "He says he's my friend, but sometimes I don't know if I ever believed him. You know? I'm just a job to him, anyway."

"Why don't you talk it over with Sarajane?" The other voice called me Sarajane. Tina always called me S.J. "She's your friend, maybe the nicest one you ever had."

There was a pause and then Tina laughed. It sounded like a bark. "I never *had* any other," she said.

"She likes you," the other voice said.

"Maybe," Tina answered, thoughtfully. "Maybe she does. Tonight, when she thought I wasn't coming over . . . she was really uptight . . ."

"Yes . . ."

"Ahhh . . . nobody really ever cares," she said.

"You don't believe that any more," the other voice answered.

"Maybe another time I'll go back," Tina said. "Not now. This is the best place . . ."

"You ought to talk to Sarajane," the other voice said. "You ought to tell her about it, because she's going to find out sometime."

"Maybe not," from Tina.

"Maybe not," the other voice said, "but even so, you should trust her enough to tell her."

"Yeah, trust," Tina said. "Frances used to say that to us kids. '*Trust* me,' she said. 'I won't hurtcha . . .'"

The other voice answered firmly: "*Forget* about Frances. That's all over now. Forget Frances, forget Georgia, forget Marty, forget them all." The rocking began as Tina chanted the names of all the people she had to forget. "Forget" was spoken to the wall and the person's name was spoken toward me. I could tell from the louder and softer sounds the way she was rocking. And the bed squeaked. The whole thing reminded me of music. And after a little while, Tina had rocked herself to sleep.

I lay in the same position with my eyes closed. The more I found out, I thought, the more secrets I had to keep. Tina had secrets . . . but that was different, she wasn't spying on me. I felt like the biggest cheat of all.

Noise from the kitchen woke me early Saturday morning and when I went in there, Pa and Bo and Tina were sitting at the table. Katie was at the stove. And all of them were dressed.

" 'Morning, Sara," Pa said. "How'd you manage to sleep with all that sun pouring in there?"

"Guess I was tired," I said, going over to the refrigerator. I poured some juice into a little glass.

"Can we go swimming today, Sarajane?" Bo asked.

"Probably gonna rain," Pa said.

"No, it ain't," Bo said.

"*Isn't*," I corrected.

"Even Sarajane says so," Bo said.

I yawned, too tired to even correct him again. "Is Ma still sleeping?" I asked.

"For a change," Pa answered.

"Isn't this her morning to do breakfast?"

Pa put down his coffee cup. "Well, I was up and she could use the rest. But I'm going to have some extra help this morning, so it won't be bad!" He smiled at Tina.

"You working breakfast this morning?" I asked Tina.

"Yeah," she said. "Why not. I was up."

"It was Katie's idea," Pa said. "And Tina liked it. Right?"

"Sure," Tina said.

"Katie asked Tina? To help this morning?" I asked. But since that's what they just got finished saying, nobody answered me.

Pa got up from the table and brought his dishes to the sink. "Let's go then," he said to the girls. "You're on dish-detail, Sara."

I nodded and watched them as they went out the screen door. "See ya later," I called. And Tina waved.

Betty Harmon phoned later on in the morning. She had a bunch of shorts and T-shirts that her brother had outgrown and her mother thought that maybe Bo could use them. I said sure, I'd be down to get them. I like chores that take me out of the house for a while so most of the time I volunteer to run errands.

I was at the Land's End section of the woods when I found myself almost face-to-face with Mr. Hopper. He had just gone swimming, I guess, because his hair was all wet and he had a big beach towel wrapped around his shoulders.

He looked away from me. I figured he was embarrassed about that day we went fishing, so I said, "Hi, Mr. Hopper."

"Hello, there, Sarajane," he answered and smiled a little. Then he looked down again. "Not angry at me, are you?" He sounded like a little boy. Like Bo.

"Gee, no, why should I be?"

"Kind of let you down a little," he said.

"No, you didn't. It was a rotten day for fishing."

He nodded. "Yes," he said, "it was a rotten day." And he continued walking toward his cabin.

Chapter Twelve

T.G.I.F.—"Thank God it's Friday"—We used to say that at the end of every week in school. Pa used to say it in the winter time, too, but *he* meant that's when he'd work harder, because business would pick up on the weekends. During the week in the off-season, he said he'd sit around and count the salt and pepper shakers.

Anyway, T.G.I.F. was what I was thinking about, since it was Friday, when Mama called from the restaurant.

"Sara, I need you to work lunch today. I had a reservation for eight, that was the Northport Women's Club, but I just got another one for ten, and with the regular crowd . . . Well, I could use you. You wanna get Bo and come on down here?"

"Sure," I told her. "But the laundry's not through yet."

"That's okay," she said, "forget the laundry, this is more important. See you soon, honey."

Bo had wet his bed a lot this summer, so we were always washing sheets. But we were lucky—Martha Beck had given us a bunch of old sheets from the Meridian that she was going to throw out. There wasn't anything wrong with them, they had just turned a little gray, but she said the best motel in town had to have clean-looking sheets, so she gave the old ones to us.

Bo had a fit when I told him I wouldn't be taking him to the lake that afternoon, and I wondered if he'd carry on like that when he got old enough to do his share of work like everyone else.

When we got there, I found Tina waiting tables. It was her first time and she was really trying hard. She wasn't smiling or even stopping for a minute. She came in and out of the kitchen with her orders and she carried big trays and she kept her mouth in a straight line the whole time. You could hardly even see her lips.

"Want me to wait, too?" I asked Ma.

"No, Sara, I want you to help Katie with the salads. That's all they're ordering today, it seems. I want all that lettuce washed and torn, I want those radishes cut into roses, I want . . ."

"I know, okay," I said. "Where are the orders?"

"Next to the plates over there. Here, Bo," she said, handing him a sandwich.

"Aw, it's chicken," he said.

It was a busy lunchtime. We all worked hard—people were still coming in at one-thirty. But by two o'clock, the big parties had left and the rush was over. There were just three or four tables being used.

"Can I wait on those alone, Miz Punch?" Tina asked. "Please?"

"No, Tina, that's too much. This is only your first time. You do two and Earl will do two."

"That's silly, let Earl go, I can—"

Just then, the kitchen door swung open. It was pushed so hard, we all turned around and stopped talking—Pa, Mama, Tina—all of us stopped what we were doing and saying and stood there looking at Mrs. Harris, who had come in. She had put her hands behind her back and her face was very red.

"Oh, please excuse me . . ." she began, "I'm sorry to interrupt, but . . ."

"It's all right, Mrs. Harris," Ma said. "Would you like to sit down? Care for a cold drink?"

"No, no. Thank you . . . I was looking for . . . I need Tina to . . . Tina, Mrs. Samios needs you to watch the twins. She wants you to take them down to the lake. To swim." She looked at Tina only once, when she called her name, and then she looked at the floor.

"Yeah, well, I can't. I'm waiting tables. I'm busy," Tina said, and picked up her order pad.

"No, *Tina!*" Mrs. Harris said. She didn't yell, but it seemed louder than she'd ever talked before. "You've got to go take care of the Samios boys."

Tina looked up at her and stuck out her jaw. "Forget it!" she said. "I said, I'm busy!"

Nobody said anything. Ma started to put her hand on Tina's shoulder, then stopped.

Mrs. Harris took a deep breath. "Go on down to the Shoreline, Tina. Now!" She barked out the "now!".

For a second, I thought Tina was going to hit her. Or throw something. Her arm jerked up, like it does when you're going to take aim at something, but then, just as quickly, she put it down. She gave Mrs. Harris a tough look, and she kept on looking the whole time she was taking off her apron and hanging it up. She was still looking at her while she went out the swinging door into the dining room, and almost bumped into it. But she did go.

"Well, come on, folks," Pa said, after a minute. "Let's get cracking here. Earl, you take those four tables left, okay?"

"There's only two, Mr. Punch. Here's the dessert order for the ones left."

"Flo?" Pa said, handing them to her.

We had forgotten Mrs. Harris was still there, until

she suddenly burst into tears. She put her hands up to cover her face and stood there sobbing in the middle of the kitchen floor.

"Kate, do these desserts," Ma said, handing the orders behind her to Katie, who went quietly to work. Ma put her arm around Mrs. Harris's shoulder and led her to the table where they both sat down.

"I'm—I'm sorry, I know you're busy . . ." Mrs. Harris mumbled through tears.

"It's all right. Your timing was good," Ma smiled kindly, "the rush is over. You tell me what it is."

Mrs. Harris looked around at Pa and Katie and Bo. Just then, Earl came in and began to putter around the counter.

Ma looked, too. "All right, come on out front. We'll sit in the window seat in the corner. No one'll bother us and we won't bother anyone. Come on." She got up and took Mrs. Harris's arm.

They were almost at the door, when Mrs. Harris turned back to me. "Can Sarajane come, Mrs. Punch? I guess she ought to hear this, too . . ."

Ma nodded at me. "Sara?" she said, which meant, *let's go*.

No one was sitting in the window seat and the drapes were drawn so we couldn't be seen from the outside. Ma handed Mrs. Harris one of the cloth napkins to use as a handkerchief, since she didn't seem to have any tissues. Mrs. Harris covered her whole face with it while she finished crying. I started wiggling, but Ma didn't say a word.

Finally, Mrs. Harris said, "I gave Mrs. Samios money and told her to pay Tina for taking care of the twins."

I said, "Huh?"

"Hush, Sarajane," Ma said.

"No, it's all right . . ."

Mrs. Harris said, wiping her eyes. "What I meant was, I asked if Tina could watch the boys. To get her out of here, so I could . . . I could talk to you. Both."

I opened my mouth but Ma quickly put her hand on my arm and I closed it.

"Jim's in New York . . ." Mrs. Harris went on, "and I just couldn't stay alone . . ."

If she didn't say what it was soon I thought I'd burst.

"Mr. Gerardi called this morning. Tina's mother wants her back. Definitely."

Ma sucked in air and made a noise.

"Why?" I yelled.

Ma said, "Shh."

"She wants her, I don't know. She's done everything she's supposed to do . . . she has a job, she's living alone now . . . This man—" Mrs. Harris stopped talking and looked at me, then Ma. Neither of us said anything. "Anyway, she's living by herself and as long as she can support Tina, Mr. Gerardi thinks it's okay for her to go back. Tina doesn't know, of course . . . I just found out . . ."

"What if Tina doesn't want to go back!" I said.

"It's her *mother*, Sarajane . . . They listen to the

child, but it's not up to the child . . . Anyway, maybe she will want to go back. I just don't think she'll be . . . It's not the right place . . ."

I closed my eyes.

"Mr. Gerardi says we'll get a formal written notice ten days before they take her . . . away. We can contest it . . ."

"Well, then!" Mom cried.

"He says it's our right. We have to respond right away and then we have a conference with a lawyer we pick and if they still decide to take her we can appeal . . ."

" 'Contest' means you can say you don't want her to go, right?" I said, trying to piece it all together in my head. "You can say that in court and then they let you keep her, right?"

Mrs. Harris sighed. "We can say that at a special conference . . . but it could go against us anyway. All we'd do is delay it . . . and she'd end up back there anyway. I have to talk to Jim . . ." Mrs. Harris blew her nose, took a deep breath and sat up straight. "It'll be a *gradual* going-away," she went on. "Tina will make a couple more day-visits, then there's a trial period."

"What kind of trial period?" Ma asked.

"Well, she'll stay there for a while. A week maybe. Let them both get used to each other. Then at the end of the week, Tina'll come back here, visit there some more, and finally, I guess she'll just . . . stay there. If it works out. See—the case has to be reviewed by the Family Court, but Mr. Gerardi says sometimes they don't even review it until the child has already been returned to the parent. That is, if things are going okay there . . ."

"Really?" Ma said. I thought, *this* is the best place of all . . . Tears began to run down my cheeks but I didn't make any sound.

"Do you know Tina hasn't lived with that woman since she was six years old?" Mrs. Harris said to Ma. "Why does she want her back *now*? Just now, when things are beginning to work out for her? Do you know she's been in four other homes? And she's only eleven?"

Ma ran her fingers through her hair, pulling a strand back over her ear. "Wipe your face, Sarajane," she said, handing me another napkin. "When are you going to tell her?"

"Well, I have to tell her soon. She's got to go in for another visit. She's got to know what's happening . . ."

"When will the trial period be?" I asked.

"I guess pretty soon, if things go . . . well, Mr. Gerardi said. I don't think he's too happy about it, but of course, he wouldn't say . . ." She turned her hands, palms up, and looked toward the ceiling, like she was praying or something. "I couldn't get hold of Jim, I just had to tell someone before I told Tina. I'm sorry, but you had to know anyway, so I just—"

"It's all right, don't give that a thought," Ma said, taking Mrs. Harris's hand in both of hers. "Of course, we'd want to know. And we won't say anything to anyone until it becomes a fact."

Mrs. Harris stood up. "Thank you. Thank you, Sarajane. I feel a little better . . . I guess I just have to get used to this . . . Then I can tell Tina . . ." We watched her walk out through the front door.

Ma put her arms around me. "I'm sorry, honey. I'm sorry for the Harrises, for that little girl . . . for you . . ."

Then I could cry out loud.

"I can't work tonight," I told Ma as she was getting ready to leave for the dinner shift.

"Why not?" The hand automatically reached for my forehead like it always does if I say something a little unusual. "Feel all right?"

"No," I said, grabbing the excuse. "I feel sick." I didn't know if Mrs. Harris had told Tina yet, but whether she had or she hadn't, *I* still wasn't supposed to know anything about *anything* and I just couldn't stand to see her with all of that inside me. I couldn't. I couldn't see her.

"Sarajane?"

"What, Mama?"

"You don't have a fever."

"But I feel awful."

"Want to go up and lie down?" she asked. I nodded. "Come on, Bo! Come with me!" she called out the back door. "Katie?" up the stairs. "Let's go, hon!" Back to me: "You be all right by yourself?"

"Yes."

"Call if you need me." And in a minute, everyone was gone.

I went to bed and slept until the next morning. I didn't even hear anyone come in from work.

The next few days were awful. I didn't want to see Tina because everytime I looked at her face I felt like saying something about what I knew. Or crying. Or both. I didn't even know if she'd been told about going back to live with her mother. She sure didn't let on.

It was a good thing we *were* busy in the restaurant, because we didn't get a chance to talk or be alone. A couple of times she'd say things like, "Hey, what's wrong with *you*!" or "Man, you look like you just pulled your face out of a puddle of crud!" but that's about all.

On Sunday I yelled at her. I hated that but I couldn't help it. She said, "Come on, S.J., rush is over. Let's grab a swim!"

"No," I said. "I'm tired."

"Me, too. We'll feel better after a swim."

"No," I said.

"Oh, come *on*, jeez, you're a drag lately!"

And then I snapped. "Would you just leave me alone, for cryin' out loud!"

She didn't answer, but she stayed away from me after that.

Monday was our day off and I was dreading it,

hoping and expecting she would come over and afraid she would.

When she didn't, I thought it was because of the way I behaved toward her over the weekend and then I felt worse.

I walked down to the lake and visited each of the motels. We hardly ever saw our friends during the summer, everyone was so busy at their own places.

I looked for Betty Harmon over at the Land's End, but she was out giving sailing lessons. Rosemarie Rice was doing her macrame with that silly lady Alice that I waited on and her little girl.

"Want to do macrame?" Rosemarie called. While Alice and her little girl were looking down at their knots, she made a face at me that said, "Help! These two are turkeys!" I smiled but I didn't feel like helping. Especially *Alice*. So I waved at Rosemarie and kept on going.

Everyone was doing something . . . Harriet Harmon was taking care of two little boys who were staying at Land's End, Neddy Sumner was mowing . . .

I didn't really want to play with anybody anyway. I found Martha Beck coming out of one of the Meridian rooms with a pile of towels.

"Hi, Sarajane. Day off? Sure, it is, it's Monday," she said, answering her own question. "How'd you like to spend it working here? Cora didn't show up today." Cora Zabriskie graduated from Meridian High in June and was marking time before college working at the Meridian Motel.

I shook my head. "I just don't feel like it Mrs. Beck. But I will another time . . ." Any other time I would've been glad to help out. I liked it at the Meridian. But not then . . . not that day.

"It's okay, honey, we'll manage," she said.

She was busy, so I went over to Jessie Hart's. Jessie was in her little office with her feet propped up on a stool. She had a newspaper on her lap but she wasn't reading it.

"Well, Sarajane Veronica! How are you?" she said when she saw me come in.

I laughed. "That's not my middle name," I said.

"I know, but doesn't it sound pretty? Like poetry: Sa-ra-jane-ver-*on*-i-ca . . . played on her har-*mon*-i-ca . . ."

"Aw, Jessie . . ."

"You know what? You look blue. You shouldn't be blue. How old are you, ten?" she asked.

What did that have to do with anything? "Eleven," I said.

"Well, you're eleven years old, it's a beautiful summer day, you have some time to yourself . . . What could make you look so down in the dumps?" She leaned back and smiled a big smile. Instead of making me feel better I felt worse.

"Nothing . . ." I said. "I feel okay. I'll see ya."

"All right. Sarajane Ver-*on*-i-ca . . ." she was still chanting it as I went out. Everybody seemed to be saying the wrong thing to me. Everything either made me mad or sad.

The Shoreline. I got there after all. I found Mrs. Harris hanging clothes outside on a little clothesline, the kind that folds up. She must've brought it from the city . . .

"Hi, Mrs. Harris . . ." I said.

"Hi, Sarajane."

I kept sneaking looks toward the cabin, but I couldn't see anything.

"She's not here. She's visiting her mother today," Mrs. Harris said, even though I hadn't asked. Makes me feel a little creepy when grownups do that, like read your mind.

"Oh."

"Jim and I didn't tell her until the night . . . you know, last Friday? I waited for him to get home." She hung up a pair of Tina's shorts on the line. They were pink, with little daisies on them. The ones Tina had made fun of at the fireworks show.

"What did she say?" I asked.

"She never said a thing to you, huh?" Mrs. Harris asked. I shook my head. "I don't know, Sarajane, I just don't know." She kept on hanging clothes—bend, pick up, drape over, clip; bend, pick up, drape, clip . . . "I just had the feeling if I told Tina she was going to live with her mother a month ago she'd've had some kind of screaming fit. Either joy or maybe, anger, something—I just have that feeling. And even then, I *still* wouldn't have known what she was really thinking . . ." Mrs. Harris did what she always did when she talked about Tina—looked very far away,

.156.

like she was talking to herself. But she stopped hanging clothes. She just kept smoothing out the same shirt that was already hung up. "But she didn't do anything. She said, 'Oh. Yeah?' just like that. With no expression or anything. 'Oh. Yeah?' And she hasn't mentioned it since." Bend, pick up . . .

"Are you going to 'contest' it?"

"Don't know, Sarajane."

"Thank you," I said, not knowing what to say.

"I'll tell her you were here . . . I don't know what time she'll be back," Mrs. Harris said.

"You don't have to," I said, and headed for the water. I felt like I was going to cry again, dammit!

I rubbed my eyes and began to walk to the top of the hill. Halfway up, Mr. Hopper crossed my path, heading toward the water. In one hand he had his fishing rod and in the other, his green tackle box. He looked up at me for just a second—smiled at me for just a second—and walked on.

I went on to the top and watched him pick his way over the pebbles until he reached the Kozy rowboat. The oars were there, lying across the seats. He put the tackle box on the bottom of the boat and the rod next to the oars. He got in and pushed off at the same time, not even bothering to put the oars in the oarlocks first. As he lifted one up to fit it into the lock, he caught me watching him. I couldn't see his eyes, but I could tell, and for one instant, his body froze, his arm holding the oar, which was sticking straight up from the bottom of the boat like a mast.

Then he just slid it into the lock and rowed away. His was the only boat I could see on the lake . . .

I turned away and went on to where the last cabin in the farthest group of cabins sits in some marsh next to the shore. Every year Pa says that place is going to go under but it never does. Its little dock hung out over the water but you could never dive from it, it was too shallow. It was just a little boat dock. With no boat.

I sat on it and cried till it was time to go back.

I didn't see Tina until Tuesday night when we both went in for the dinner shift. She said "Hi" and I said "Hi", and then we just did our own work thing. When we were finished, she took off her apron, hung it up and slammed out the kitchen door.

Wednesday the same thing happened. I didn't see her until dinner, even though the Samios twins were over all day playing with Bo. At the end of the night, she hung up her apron and slammed out again. That door went *crack* every time Tina closed it. Only this time, she came back. It was just a few minutes later, but she was back. She came inside and slammed the door the same way. She stood there for a few minutes and Pa said, "You forget something, Tina?" but she just shook her head. Finally, she walked over to me.

"I wanna ask you somethin'," she said. She sounded like she was going to hit me.

"What?" I said and waited but she didn't say anything. She just stared at me, moving her upper and lower teeth back and forth. So I didn't say anything either.

"I just wanna ask you. I wanna know . . . What'd I do to you, anyway?" She was breathing very hard, like she just ran a long way.

I coughed. "Nothing. You didn't do nothing. *Anything*, I mean."

"Oh, yeah, then how come. Then why is it you're not talkin' to me any more."

"I am. You haven't come around, is all," I said.

"Well I haven't come around because you're not talking to me," she said.

I felt better and worse at the same time. "I just . . . I . . ." I shrugged my shoulders. "I haven't had much to say," I told her. It sounded whiney.

She looked down at her feet, which were bare. Her toenails were painted. "I got somethin' to say," she said. I *thought* she said.

"What?"

"I said, I got somethin' to say. What's the matter, you deaf, too?" This was louder and Katie turned around. "Come on outside," Tina said.

We walked out together and sat on the hammock in the back. Pa followed us out carrying the garbage so we didn't say anything until he was back inside.

"I wanna tell you something, okay?" she said.

"Okay," I said. My whole head was bursting.

" 'Member I said my mother was in Europe?" she said. I just nodded at her but I didn't look at her. I hated myself for getting weepy again. I bit my lower lip hard, real hard, and stopped my eyes from filling up.

"Well, uh. She's not in Europe. That was a lie."

"Oh," I whispered.

"Whaddya mean 'oh'?" She cried. "Don't you care that I lied to you?"

I shook my head. I could hardly speak. "Anyway," I managed, "you're telling me now, so that's like you cancel out the lie."

I guessed that was a good thing to say because she calmed down. "Don't you wanna know where she is?"

"Yes . . ."

"She's in New York. She's always been there. But I didn't live with her," she said.

I had to say all the right things or she would think it was strange but I felt like *I* was lying, saying them. "How come?" I asked.

"I'm a foster kid. That's what they call kids whose mother can't keep 'em. Or father. I live in foster homes. That's what the Harrises are—my foster parents." She waited for me to say something, I guess, but I didn't, so she went on. " 'Member I told you about my uncle? Well, he's not my uncle, he's a guy who was with my mother for a while but not any more. His name's Marty. *And he doesn't own a department store!*" She started to laugh and so did I. We laughed and laughed while the hammock swung back and forth.

"But the thing is . . ." she finally continued, "my

mother wants me to come back to live with her now. She wants me. She asked for me. Paulo, you know, Paulo Gerardi? Well, he's not my friend, he's my case worker. He's the one who puts me in the homes and he's the one who stays in touch with my mother and the Family Court and all those bozos . . . Y'know, he put me in this one home . . ." she started to laugh again. "The woman's name was Frances, uh, I forget her last name, she was such a witch . . ." Tina got up from the hammock and sat on the grass next to it, rocking back and forth. Like she did when she talked to her locket. ". . . she had these kids, four of them besides me, one was black . . . Anyway . . . she always hit us white kids with this bamboo backscratcher she had, but she always hit the black kid with a brush, a hairbrush. It was almost funny, we used to laugh. Because she'd want to hit the black kid and the backscratcher would be sitting right there in front of her, and she'd go looking for the brush. One day I pulled the brush out of her hand and smacked her across the thigh with it. Hard. Next day, zap, I was sent away. Slept at Paulo's the next night. Coupla nights. Till he found another place for me."

"Why did she, uh, how come she had you live with her if she already had four kids?" I asked.

"Oh, well, see the state gives you money to keep a foster kid. I don't know how much, but you can bet ol' Frances didn't spend it on us! Before Frances, I lived with Georgia and Uri."

"Uri?"

"Yeah. They were nice . . . They had no other kids, foster kids or real kids . . ."

"What happened with them?" I asked. I felt so free, I could ask and ask and ask . . .

"I threw a plate at Georgia," she said, quietly.

"Why?" I asked, ready to laugh. I don't know why it sounded funny, but I thought it was supposed to be a funny story.

"How should I know, I was only six," she said. "That's when I got moved again and went to Frances. Know where else I went? The Cen-ter for Pre-ven— wait a minute—for Preventive Psychiatry. How's that!"

"What is it?"

"Don't ask me. Paulo says that's where they send kids who can't make it in another home. I went up there twice. It was dumb."

"Where else?" I said.

"Where else did I live?"

"Yeah."

"Well, after Frances I was supposed to go back to my mother, but that didn't work out, so I went to, um, the Hollingsworths. Right. The Hollingsworths. I *hated* them!"

"Why?"

"I just did. So, zap, Paulo pulls me out again. just like I knew he would."

"Do you like him?" I asked.

"Who, Paulo? I dunno . . . I never thought about it . . . he's okay, I guess."

"Tina?"

"What."

"Why didn't you ever tell me? Right away, I mean? Why did you make up about your mother being rich and in Europe and everything?"

"You mad?"

"Hey, no! I'm not mad . . ."

"S.J. . . . I have to go away soon, y'know?"

"When? How soon?"

"Well first I have to go live with my mother for a week. Paulo says it's like a test. To see how it works. See, my mother remembers me when I was six years old, but she doesn't know me now. I mean, I saw her all the time while I was living in those other homes, but only for a day here and there. So now she has to get to know me and I have to get know her. All over again. So Paulo has to see how it works. We have to see how it works. Maybe we'll hate each other.

" 'Member when I told you I went to New York and did all those things, the Empire State Building and everything?"

"Uh huh."

"Well, that was a lie . . . I was really going to see Paulo. Then later on I went to see my mother, too."

"Oh."

"Jim drives me into the city and we take a subway to Paulo's office at the Department. Then he takes me to my mother. That's how we've been doing it."

"Did the Harrises ever meet your mother?"

"Nah. She never saw any of the people I lived with. Why were you mad at me?"

The question took me by surprise. Tina had told me the truth. At last. And all the reasons I had to stay away from her disappeared. She was my best best friend in the whole world. Except now *I* had secrets. I just knew deep inside I could never tell her that I knew practically everything she just told me.

"I wasn't mad at you," I said softly. "I was mad at myself, and so I didn't want to have a friend while I was mad at myself."

She looked right into my face. "I know just how that feels," she said. And we sat there, me in the hammock, her on the grass, until I heard Ma call from inside the kitchen.

"Well!" she said loudly, "that clean-up took a lot longer than I figured! Guess we better get Sarajane and go on home!" The lights from the kitchen went out instantly and the whole family filed out the back door.

I hoped Ma fooled Tina, but she didn't fool me. They must've been through a long time before. Ma just made everybody stay inside twiddling their thumbs until Tina and I were finished talking! Ma is a very smart lady.

Chapter Thirteen

After that, Tina went into New York once or twice a week for a while. She always came back the same day and she only missed working dinners at the restaurant a couple of times. That was because Mr. Harris's shift was different, he was on the four-to-midnight, so he picked her up at midnight and brought her home.

She never seemed to be in an especially bad mood after these visits, but she wasn't jumping around, either. Anyway, she didn't talk about them to me and I wondered if she was telling it all to the locket.

She never did stay overnight there until it was time for the trial. That's what we called it—"the trial." It sounded like a TV program and made it very exciting. Well, kind of exciting.

"The trial" was supposed to last a week. It came toward the end of August. Tina and I slept together in the tent the night before she was supposed to leave. I fell asleep right away so I don't know if she even talked to her locket or not. It was a little bit sad that night, before we went to sleep. Mrs. Harris kept after Tina a lot, asking her if she had enough to eat, even though Tina said yes about a million times; and she asked if Tina was dressed warm enough and it really wasn't that cool out, stuff like that. Mr. Harris didn't say hardly anything, but he kept coming out to check the tent before we fell asleep and once he even woke me up, checking. He said he was real sorry and didn't come back after that. At least, I don't think so. I was out like a light.

Mr. Harris drove Tina in at about two-thirty in the afternoon, and this time she'd stay for the whole week. That morning, we went in to help Ma with the breakfast shift and Katie made Tina a cheese omelet. Tina didn't even ask her to, she just did it on her own. It was funny, because before we went to work, Mrs. Harris made us a real big breakfast and I knew Tina wasn't hungry, but she ate Katie's omelet like she was starving.

I never talked to Katie about Tina, so I didn't know what was on Katie's mind. Maybe Ma had explained a little to her. Or maybe Katie just changed her mind about Tina all by herself, I don't know. Sometimes I had to remind myself that Katie was really only nine, and not thirty or something.

In the afternoon we went swimming. We took Bo and the Samios twins. And when it was time for Tina to get dressed and get ready to go, the twins gave her a hug.

"Ah," she said, pushing them a little, "I'm comin' back. Don't get mushy."

"What day? Wednesday? Will it be Wednesday?" one of the twins asked. Teddy! It was Teddy, it wasn't Georgie's voice, I knew that well enough!

"Yeah, probably next Wednesday," Tina said. She didn't seem surprised but maybe he talked to her more. I had begun to think he couldn't talk at all.

"Bring us back something!" That was Georgie, no question about it.

"What should I bring back, a motorcycle?" Tina said. "Should I rip one off and drive it back here?"

"Yeah, yeah!" Georgie shrieked, but Teddy tugged at her towel. "Next Wednesday?" he said in a little voice. "Tina?"

"Yeah, Ted," Tina answered and patted his head. "See ya next week, S.J.!" she called to me. "Don't do anything I wouldn't do!"

"Yeah, name one thing!" I called back to her. "Have a good time!"

I got a call Friday night. It was late, after we got

home from the restaurant. Hardly anybody called us that late because people in this town go to bed early during the season or, if they were like Pa and Ma and worked late, they'd go to bed right after that to get up early the next day.

Ma jumped out of her skin and ran to the phone. I heard her say, "Hello? Tina, wha—?" and I was right over there, pulling on her. She shook my hand away, made a face, and went on talking.

"Well, yes, but is anything wrong? . . . No, no, but are you all right . . .? It's . . . no, it's all . . . Really, Tina, it's okay. Just a minute." She handed me the phone.

"Tina?"

"Hey, S.J.! Knew you'd just be getting home . . ."

"Yeah, just. Why you calling?"

There was a pause. "Uh . . . I just, um, I had this idea . . ."

"What?" I asked.

"Could you . . . Would you wanna . . . Hey, how about you coming in here to visit me overnight?"

It was my turn for a pause. I never expected anything like that, it really took me by surprise. I looked at Ma, but that was no help since she hadn't heard what Tina wanted. I guess a lot of things went through my mind then. The first thing was, wow, I get to go to New York! And then I thought, I can't, I have to work. What would they do without me? Then: what's Tina's mother like? Would she want me?

"Did you ask your mother?" I said. "Did she say it would be okay?"

"She doesn't care," was the answer, but before I could say anything, Tina said, "Yeah, I asked her, sure. It's okay with her."

"Well, just a minute," I told her and covered the receiver with my hand. "Ma? Tina wants to know if I can visit her in New York."

Mama looked over at Pa, who was holding a sleepy Bo. Katie put her hand up to her mouth. Everybody but Bo looked at me.

"Hey, this is costing me money!" Tina's voice yelled in my ear. "You coming in or not?"

"Listen," I said, "I don't know. I have to work, y'know. The weekend's here. Can I call you back?" Pa rolled his eyes. "I mean, I guess we have to talk about it, okay?"

There was a sigh on the other end of the phone. "When will you know?" she asked.

"Well..." I didn't know what to tell her.

"Okay, look," she said. "When you find out, go tell Emily. She'll call me. You could drive in with Jim, like I do. But will you know by tomorrow?"

"Oh, sure. Are you ... doing okay?" I asked.

Pause. "Yeah!"

"Well, if I can't come, don't be mad or anything. I ... have a lot to do here, you know how it is ... and it costs money ..." I said, looking at Pa, who nodded.

"It won't cost you anything if you come in with

.169.

Jim and go home with him. We have food, ha ha!"

"What do you mean, 'ha ha'?"

"Well, right now the food is two cans of Campbell's Tomato Soup and a box of, um, let's see . . . Corn Toasties."

"Is that all you have?" I asked.

"Yup, but it's okay, Welfare check comes tomorrow, if we don't get ripped off. Hey, try to come, willya?"

I said I would and hung up. I wasn't sure I wanted to, but I felt like I had to. Maybe that's almost the same thing.

"She wants you to come to New York?" Ma said.

"Yah."

"No sir," Pa said, definitely. "You're not goin' to New York, it's expensive, I need you here, and I don't trust anybody in that city, let alone my own daughter! Forget it."

"You don't trust me?" I asked.

"I don't trust *other* people," Pa said. "I don't want anything happening to you."

I looked at Ma. It was her turn.

"Wait a minute, Mike . . ." she began.

"Now, Flo, don't start. I don't want her in the city, especially without us, and who knows what that kid's home life is like . . ." Pa said.

"Do you want to go, Sarajane?" Ma asked.

"Yes."

"Let's do this," Ma said. "Let's call Mr. Gerardi in the morning and see what he thinks."

"Flo, it's the *weekend!*" Pa said.

Ma put her thumbnail up to her lower lip. "Yes . . ." she said, "but Sarajane could go on Sunday, that's not *too* busy, and Monday, she'll be off anyway. She could be back on Monday night."

"I don't *understand* you," Pa said. "We're not just talking about a night in Northport, Flo. This is New York City, Flo. And what about where that kid's living now . . ."

"Mike," Ma said softly, "it's *Tina*. Look at all she's done for us down at the place . . ."

"I paid her," Pa said.

"What she was worth?" Ma asked him.

Pa laughed a little. "I couldn't *afford* what she was worth . . ."

"You see?" Ma said. "She and Sarajane are so good for each other . . ."

I walked between them. "You guys are talking about me like I'm not even here," I said, and they laughed again.

"You've been a good team this summer," Ma said, smoothing my hair. "I want things to work out for Tina. You know, you could take Mr. Harris's work number with you and call him if you need somebody . . ."

"Awww, I won't need anybody . . ." I said.

"Why don't we just see what Mr. Gerardi says in the morning?" Ma said, "and get some sleep now!"

Ma and I went over to the Harrises right after

breakfast. Mrs. Harris perked up when we told her what we wanted.

"I'll call him right away," she said. She had two numbers for Mr. Gerardi, his home phone and his work phone. He was at work.

"I'd like to talk to him myself," Ma said, and Mrs. Harris explained and handed her the phone.

After Ma told him that Tina had called and what she wanted, she said, "We're a little worried about Sarajane staying there by herself, and we wanted to know what you thought."

Then she listened while Mr. Gerardi told her. She kept nodding and nodding. Finally she said, "Let me talk to my daughter and my husband and I'll call you back. Will you be in your office all day? . . . Well, then I'll leave a message there and you'll be able to get it to Tina? . . . Fine . . ."

I motioned for her to give me the phone and she did. "Mr. Gerardi? This is Sarajane Punch . . ."

"Hi, S.J.," he said.

"Hi. Listen, whatever we do, please call Tina right away and tell her so she doesn't think I forgot . . . okay. Promise?" I asked.

"Don't worry about it. I just told your mother I'll be out of the office but I'll keep calling in until I get a message from you and I'll let her know, don't worry. Ask your mother what I said, okay? 'Bye, S.J." He hung up.

I looked at Ma and waited for her to speak. So did Mrs. Harris.

"He thinks it's a good idea," she said. "He's been talking to Tina every day and he thinks she misses us all, though she won't say. But she has been behaving herself." She turned to Mrs. Harris. "It seems Mrs. Gogolavsky's job fell through . . ." Mrs. Harris took a deep breath . . . "but she is on some sort of public assistance, so it's all right . . ." Mrs. Harris let out the breath and sat down. ". . . I would think the parent had to have a job before they'd let them have the child back . . ." Ma said, thoughtfully.

"I guess Welfare's all right," Mrs. Harris sighed and looked past us.

"He thinks you'll be fine," Mama said to me. "Tina knows her way around, the mother's all right—Most of all, he thinks it'll do Tina a lot of good for you to do this. 'Come onto her turf' was the way he put it. In other words—Meridian is *your* territory, *your* place, so it's your advantage, like in a game. But New York is *Tina's* place, so she'll have the advantage—taking care of *you*, showing *you* around, and also . . ."

"Also?" I asked.

"Also, she'll see she really has a friend who comes to her when she calls. Understand?"

"Yes," I answered. I guess I understood that right from the beginning.

Chapter Fourteen

Patrolmen work on Sundays, too, in fact right through the weekend, just like restaurant people, so Mr. Harris went to work Sunday morning and took me with him. It was early, because he had the eight a.m. shift again. The trip took a little over an hour. I had a big vinyl hatbox with my stuff in it. Someone once left it in the restaurant and never came back for it, though we had it ready for them for weeks, maybe months. It was really nice. It looked like real leather and it had a pretty strap to carry it by. The only things it had in it when we found it were a bunch of cosmetics, all *kinds* of stuff: eyeshadow and different-color rouges and blushes and lipsticks and pencils for drawing around your eyes and everything. Pa said it probably belonged to an actress, because who else would use all that goop. Tell you who, Katie and I, that's who. When Ma and Pa finally decided it was ours, Katie and I played with the stuff all winter. Bo even played with it.

Right now, the hatbox held underwear, a nightie, a toothbrush, a pair of shorts and a top, and a dress. Just in case. In case of what, I wanted to know. Just in case, Ma said. And I had Mr. Harris's precinct number on a paper in a zippered compartment.

We swung onto a street that had a big sign on it: PLAY STREET, CLOSED TO TRAFFIC. I was about to ask Mr. Harris why he was driving onto the street, but he pulled right over to the curb at the corner.

"We're here, Sarajane," he said. "We'll walk just up the block a bit. Give me your bag." I stared as I handed him the bag.

There was a game of stickball going on in the middle of the street. Tina told me that was the only game she ever liked to play. But the children playing it didn't look like they were having a good time. They were playing in, like, slow motion. I guessed it was because it was so hot out.

There was a man. Sleeping on a stoop. He had on a short-sleeved shirt and his head was resting on his two pale arms while he slept. The position he was in was just like Bo when he sleeps.

A group of men was standing in a circle in front of the next stoop. One of them was kneeling down. I couldn't see what they were doing, but they were yelling every now and then. Mr. Harrris reached down and took my hand. With his other hand, I noticed he kept wiping his mouth.

"This is—" he started to say, but we both saw Tina at the same time. She was sitting on the stoop of one of the buildings and she was watching for us.

"Hey, S. JAAA-Y!" she called and ran down the steps to meet us.

"Hiya," I said.

"Hi, there," Mr. Harris said. He started to move toward her like he was going to hug her, maybe, but he didn't.

"Hey, Jim," she said. "How ya doin'?"

"Good," he said, nodding. "Pretty good. We miss you around the ol' cabin."

"Yeah," Tina said. And then she said, "Emily okay?" at the same time Mr. Harris said, "Emily's doing all right," and they laughed. "She, uh, misses you a lot. We'll be glad to have you back."

"They miss you at the restaurant," I said. "I work twice as hard as before."

"Yeah, well, I'll be back Wednesday," she said, looking at her sneakers.

Mr. Harris held out my hatbox. "Would you, ah, want me to bring this up there for you?" he asked me.

"Nah, I'll take it," Tina said, and he handed it to her. I could've taken it myself.

"Well!" Mr. Harris finally said, after we stood around for a while. "Guess I'll be getting over to work." But he didn't move.

"Okay. I'll probably see you tomorrow when you come for S.J.," Tina said.

"Thanks for the ride," I said to him, and then he did move back toward his car. He waved and smiled a little, but Tina had turned around and was walking back up the stairs.

"Come on," she said over her shoulder. "Let's go up."

I followed her into a dark grungy hall. Ahead of us was a long flight of steps which we began to climb.

"How high up do we go?" I asked.

"Fourth," she answered.

There was a wooden banister but when I tried to use it, it felt all sticky so I wiped my hands on my pants and climbed up without it. All around there was a funny smell.

She finally stopped climbing and walked down another dark hall to a door, partly open. "This's it," she said and kicked the door open wider.

We walked into, I guess, the living room. It was small. There were three windows on the wall facing us and they were wide open. They didn't have any screens . . . I could hear strange noises from the street below.

"Where's your mother?" I asked.

Tina jerked her head over her shoulder. "In there.

The bedroom. Usually I sleep in there, but tonight, you and me'll sleep in here. On the couch."

"Does it pull out into a bed?" I asked.

"No, but we're small, it'll be okay. Listen, if we get cramped or anything, one of us can sleep on the floor. Do you care?"

"No!" I said, quickly. " 'Course I don't care."

"Hey, Ma!" Tina called, but got no answer. "My friend is here!" Still no answer. "Come on," she said, moving toward the bedroom door.

I pulled back. "Hey, she didn't answer you. Maybe we—"

"It's okay," Tina said and opened the door. "'My friend is here," she said to someone in the room. "Can she come in?" I heard nothing, but Tina motioned me in with her head. I felt a little scared of this person I'd never seen and who was very mysterious, hiding in a bedroom, but it was like someone hypnotized me and I just walked right over to Tina and poked my head in the door.

A woman was lying on an iron bed. She was very small and very thin. She had brown hair that hung down to her shoulders in long strings. Her face was pale, pale. She had on a white sleeveless thing and her arms hung through the holes of it like it was four sizes too big for her. They were almost the same color as the dress. Or nightgown. Whatever it was. She turned her head toward me and smiled. "Hi," she said.

"Hi, Mrs. . . . uh . . ." I said, and she laughed a little. Or coughed, I wasn't sure.

"It's okay," she said, "everybody does that. You can call me Mrs. Gogo, like Bettina uses."

"Yes, ma'am," I said.

Her eyes opened wide. "You're not from around here!" she said. "Where you from?"

I looked at Tina.

"I told ya, Ma," Tina said. "S.J.'s from that town Meridian, where I been living. She came all the way down here to see me. Right?"

"Right," I said, and whispered to Tina, "did she know I was coming?"

"Yessss," she hissed. "She forgets. We're goin' out on the stoop, okay, Ma?" She asked. "You want anything before I go?"

Tina's mother moved her hand slowly on the bed, back and forth.

"I said, you want anything?" Tina repeated.

"Oh . . . no . . . No thanks. Don't go far, Bettina . . ." she said.

"Won't." I followed her out the door and down the hall again.

"Is she sick?" I asked Tina quietly. Why do people always talk quietly about sickness?

"Her?" Tina shrugged. "Sometimes. I guess. I don't know. Sometimes she lies down a lot. She always did. But she's . . . she's not sick."

When we got outside, Tina sat down on the stoop,

so I just sat down next to her. For a while we didn't say anything, just kept watching the people on the street . . . people who walked by . . .

"You don't need any TV on this street," I said. "You can just watch all the people."

"Yeah," she said. "It's better than TV because you never see the same program over. It always changes."

"So, um, how come your mother lies down a lot?" I asked.

Tina looked at me like I had asked a funny question. "*I* don't know," she said. "Maybe she just gets tired. I never thought about it."

"When you visited her before, did she always— Was she always in bed?" I asked. I wondered why anybody would stay in bed a lot if they weren't sick.

Tina scratched her head and squinted. "Yeah. I guess so. She's got some problems with her legs. Something about the veins. She doesn't eat much. She's really thin, you could see her arms . . ."

"Did she go to a doctor?" I asked.

"*I* don't know," Tina said again. "But it's good I'm here, because I do a lot for her, y'know? I can cook now. Did you know that?" I shook my head. "Well, I can. I learned how to make a lot of stuff out of things like hamburger meat. You can make hamburger meat go a long way. Bet you never tried that, huh?"

"Uh uh," I said. "I hate to cook."

"Well, I don't mind it. And I do the shopping . . . Your ma gave me some good shopping tips."

"She did?"

"Oh, yeah. I didn't know *nothing* about buying food before . . ."

"Anything," I corrected without thinking, but Tina didn't hear.

"You can make good food," she continued, "without spending a buncha money. Your ma says it takes a little *imagination*."

"Yeah, I've heard her say that . . ." I said. Ma never mentioned she taught Tina all that. Surprises . . .

"So I kind of have a job, too, just like you do at home. I really work around here . . ." She swept her arm toward the upstairs. "Hey, you wanna play stickball?"

I said, "Uh . . ." but she was already down the stoop and running toward the slow-motion game.

"Hey, Cheek, I'm playin'!" she yelled. A dark-haired boy with a broom handle in his hand turned around.

"Yeah!" he cried. "Hey, Tina's playin', you guys. Now we gotta game!"

The kids in the street suddenly seemed to move faster. They all came over as Tina and I got closer.

"This's my friend," Tina said. "Her name's S.J., she's playin', too. How many we got?"

Some kids who had been sitting on the curb got up and came over and we chose up sides. There were nine kids and the team that didn't get Tina got the extra kid. They said it was because she was the best hitter.

Stickball is played just like baseball, except with a broom handle, or mop handle, and a pink rubber ball the kids called a spaldeen. The bases were a square, drawn with chalk, on one curb for first base, a manhole cover in the middle of the street for second base, and third base was a blue Volkswagen parked across the street. A homerun was a two-sewer hit past *two* manhole covers down the middle of the street.

"One more thing," Tina said, "if the cops drive down here, throw the stick under a car."

"Why?" I asked.

"They don't like stickball," Cheek said. "They think we could break windows or hit somebody. So they take the stick away. Then we got nothin' to play with. So you quick throw the stick under a car before they see it, then they can't take it."

We played for the rest of the morning. It was fun. Nobody got a two-sewer hit. And when the blue Volkswagen drove away, we used a telephone pole for third base.

We finally stopped when the score was twenty-seven to two, favor of our team—Tina's team.

"Want lunch?" she asked.

"Sure."

"Okay, let's go up and see Ma."

Tina made soup for her mother, took some money and said we'd go out and buy lunch. We stopped at a little stand where a man was selling hot dogs under a blue and yellow umbrella. Tina said it was her treat and paid for them and we shared an orange soda. Then we went to a supermarket where she shopped like Ma does, squeezing things, and smelling things and looking at things.

"You look just like my mother," I told her.

"Oh, yeah, well, she took me shopping a couple times and showed me," Tina said.

She paid at the counter with stamps.

"Food stamps," she explained. "City's buyin' dinner." She grinned. "You can write a thank-you note to the Mayor."

"How come?"

"Well," she said, hoisting a brown bag, "Ma doesn't have a job right now, so we get Welfare checks to live on. But she'll get one, soon; she always does when she feels she can get out of bed. It'll work out. Anyway, we can eat."

We did eat, too. Tina was good. She made some dish with hamburger meat and macaroni and tomato sauce and an onion. We all ate in the bedroom with her mother and it was nice. Her mother wanted Tina to sit on the bed with her and every once in a while she'd touch her or something. We had Twinkies for dessert.

We tried to sleep on the couch but it didn't work. Tina rolled off during the night, waking *me* up, but not her. I heard the clink of a chain when she turned over on the floor and saw she was holding on tight to the locket, even while she was sleeping.

Some sounds from the kitchen woke us up the next morning. Well, it wasn't a kitchen, really, it was just a kind of place at the end of the room with a sink and refrigerator and stove. Tina's mother was standing at the sink, rattling some dishes.

Tina was over there like a flash. "Hey, don't do that," she said, taking a frying pan from her mother's hand. "*I'll* do that, you go back to bed. G'wan."

Her mother smiled weakly. "Bettina, it's all right . . . I can fix you something. I mean, I can scramble an egg . . . I'm not an invalid or anything . . ." But she let Tina support her and lead her over to the couch where I was still lying down. I quick scooted over on the couch, making room.

"I'll rub your legs for ya," Tina said, and began to massage her mother's calves and ankles.

Mrs. Gogo turned toward me. "It's poor circulation," she said. I just nodded. "See, the blood don't run so good through the veins in my legs. It's . . . hard to stay on my feet too long. I take medicine . . . I'll be better soon . . ."

"Sure you will," Tina said.

While Tina was helping her mother, I got up and washed. Then I went over to the stove and fixed breakfast with the groceries Tina had brought the day before. I was no Katie, but it was okay.

After we were finished and Tina and I had done the dishes, we sat down with Mrs. Gogo. Nobody really knew what to say. Finally, Mrs. Gogo said, "You're a nice girl, S.J. I'm glad Tina met you . . ."

"Me, too," I said.

"Me, too," from Tina.

"Tina said your folks own a restaurant. I worked in a restaurant. For a while . . . before my legs got too bad . . ."

"Oh, you did?" I asked.

"Uh huh. Not on a lake, though. You know, I've never seen a lake," she said.

"Oh."

"Nope. Never even seen one. Except in pictures, of course . . . and the movies. No, I worked in a diner down on Eleventh Avenue. Wasn't easy, working in that place. Even before my circulation got bad, my ankles would swell at the end of a day . . . Well . . . some funny things happened there, though—My friend, Vinnie, she was a waitress, too, we used to make fun of the food something awful!" Mrs. Gogo looked away from us and smiled as she began to remember. "Vinnie used to holler at the customers, 'Hurry up and eat that hash or the roaches'll beat you to it!' or 'We should charge extra for the number of legs you find in your dinner!' Chef used to get so mad . . . Bettina, you know, that's where I met your father."

"I know, Ma," Tina said.

Mrs. Gogo stopped smiling, but kept on staring into space. "Yes, baby . . . He was a regular customer at that place. Coffee every morning at ten-thirty. No doughnuts, though. I warned him about that . . . We had doughnuts older'n you, Tina . . ."

Tina smiled.

Mrs. Gogo looked down at me, sitting at her feet on the floor. "Couldn't tell you where he is today, S.J.," she said.

"And who cares," from Tina.

"He gave you a name, Bettina," her mother said.

"That nobody can pronounce," Tina said and they both laughed.

We stayed in the apartment with Tina's mother all morning and most of the afternoon. At lunch time, Tina made soup and we had breadsticks with it. Tina told her mother she thought she was eating better than she had in a long time.

At about three we went out into the street and Tina got up another stickball game. We were still playing when Mr. Harris drove up to get me at four-thirty. When we went upstairs to get my stuff and say good-bye, Mrs. Gogo held my hand real tight.

I was at work in time for the dinner shift.

Chapter Fifteen

Tina was back on Wednesday evening with Mr. Harris. Teddy Samios was practically hysterical. His mother said he hardly ate anything while Tina was away.

"Yeah, because he ate all *my* food," Bo complained.

"Did not!" Teddy yelled. Teddy *yelled*! Now, I thought, we'll never tell the twins apart.

"Um, how's your mother?" I asked Tina as we met at a waiter's station that night. She was busing for Scotty and I was busing for Earl.

"She got up today," she answered. "If she can just

get a job where she can sit down, she'll be okay. She can't stand on her feet long, y'know?"

At the end of the shift, Tina and I were both in the dining room clearing the tables at the same time, when Linda Merkel came in. Tina and I looked at each other.

"Earl's in the kitchen," Tina said, glaring at her. Just then, Earl came in through the swinging door.

"Hi, Linda," he called and went over to one of the waiters' stands.

"Hi, there, Earl," Linda called back and then she looked right at Tina. "I didn't come for Earl," she said, tilting her head and grinning. "I came for *Scotty*."

Tina's eyes flew open and so did mine! Scotty Helfin breezed out of the kitchen at that moment and waved at Linda. "Be right with you, honey," Scotty said as he took off his red waiter's jacket.

"O-kay, honey," Linda sang. "Take your time."

I covered my mouth and ran for the kitchen, followed by Tina. She was laughing, too.

"Can you figure that!" I said, choking to hold in the laughter so they couldn't hear me in the dining room.

"I'm not even gonna *try*!" Tina said, and when we stopped giggling, she said, "People will just hardly ever do what you expect."

"Paulo's coming tomorrow," Tina said to me two days later. We were at our house, finishing breakfast.

It was Pa's turn at the breakfast shift so Ma was home and Katie and Bo were, too.

"What for?" Ma asked. "Why's he coming, Tina?"

"To talk to me. Mrs. Harris says he wants to find out how I liked living in New York. With my ma." Tina fiddled with a fork. "Would you come with me while I talk to him?"

"Who, me?" I asked.

"No, Peter Pan and Wendy," she said.

"I'm not supposed to be there when you talk to him," I said.

"Show me where it says that in the rule book," Tina said.

"Why do you want *me* there?" I asked.

Tina said, "Be-*cause*."

"Oh. Okay," I said and Ma laughed.

We were waiting on the steps of Tina's cabin for Mr. Gerardi's car. Just like Tina had waited on the stoop in New York for me. I was very nervous.

"What are you going to tell him?" I asked her.

"How should I know?"

"Tina, you *have* to know," I said. "Look, what if he asks, 'Do you want to live there all the time?' What'll you say?"

"Dunno," she said, staring at the dirt.

"Yes, you *do*," I insisted. I couldn't understand why she wasn't . . . why she didn't . . . If I were Tina I'd be screaming to stay here. Why would she want to leave here, leave me, and Meridian, and the Harrises . . . Ma and Pa and *Punchy's* . . . for that small, beat-up, hot . . . place in that scary city . . . and that lady. I sighed. The lady was her mother.

"You really want to go back, don't you?" I whispered.

"You know what, S.J.?" Tina said, looking at me for the first time since we started talking. "Mr. Gerardi always called me a scrapper. A fighter, you know?"

I nodded.

"Well, he was right. I sure fought . . . Everybody. All the way. Even you, remember?"

"Yeah."

"Well . . . the way it is, see . . . I don't have to fight now. What am I gonna fight about? If I stay here . . . It's nice here. It's a good place. I don't feel . . ." she stopped, waving her hand in little circles, trying to find a word. "I don't feel *alone* here. Me against the whole crummy world."

I nodded hard. That was the truth, I knew. So how could she want to leave? "Well? So?" I asked.

"So . . . I feel that way when I'm home, too." Home. She was saying "home", and she hadn't even left yet. "My mother . . . she *wants* me. She really needs me. Y'see? So there's no reason to fight there, either. I'll be okay in either place . . ." She held her hands out with her palms up. "I don't feel like fighting anymore, do you get that, S.J.?"

Yes. No.

"Last night . . ." she went on, "Jim told me that he

and Emily could get a lawyer and have a meeting, with the agency, or a judge or something, and say they don't want me to go away. They could win, maybe."

"Yeah, Mrs. Harris mentioned something like that. They're supposed to get a letter, telling them all about it."

"Yeah, well, they asked me if they should do it."

"What'd you say?" I asked, but I knew what she'd said.

"I told them not to. It'd be a whole big scene and it really doesn't matter, see? I'll be okay." She shook her head. "Just don't feel like fighting anymore, S.J." And she grinned.

When Mr. Gerardi arrived a few minutes later, Tina asked him if I could be there while they talked. He seemed glad about that and said sure. So we walked together down toward the water. That seems to be where everybody goes to talk. After a long time of staring at the water, he said, "Good visit?"

"It was okay," Tina answered. And everybody stared at the water again.

"Wanna tell me about it?" he asked.

"*You* tell," Tina said, pointing at me.

"Me!" I can't tell how *your* visit was," I said.

Tina shrugged. "Sure you can. You were there, you saw. Tell him what you thought."

Mr. Gerardi turned sharply to Tina. "That's not fair, Tina, and you know it. I need to hear it from you. *Something* from you."

Tina suddenly sat down, crossing her legs at the same time. She bent over and began digging her fingers into the sand and the two of us, Mr. Gerardi and me, were left standing over her, staring at her scrunched body. I opened my mouth but Mr. Gerardi quick put his fingers up to his lips to shush me and went on staring at Tina.

Finally, without moving, she said, "If I have to go back to the city . . . and live with my ma . . . it'll be okay. If I have to stay here with . . . the Harrises . . . it'll be okay. But my mother needs me." She looked up then.

Mr. Gerardi smiled. "No screaming? No taking off your shoe and throwing it at me?"

Tina grinned back and shook her head.

Mr. Gerardi, looked at me. "How 'bout that, S.J.?" he said. And back to her: "Good, Tina. Very good."

When Tina finally had to leave, most of us were used to the idea. Though it still hurt. I cried a little but only when Teddy did. We knew for a long time she was going. Mrs. Harris said that even though they'd have to give up the cabin after Labor Day, maybe they'd come up on weekends in the fall till it got cold and they'd bring Tina with them, so it wouldn't really be goodbye.

The morning she went back we got up at five a.m., just the two of us, and walked down to the lake. For the first few minutes, we kidded around, but we knew we were kind of forcing it, being funny, so we just didn't say anything. The sun was already up when we got to the beach, the ground was wet, and birds were making a big racket, but it was like there weren't any people at all, except us. Some ducks swam by, real close to the shore. They were all brown—females.

"Wish we had some bread," I whispered.

"Huh?"

"I said, I wish we had some bread. For the ducks."

"Oh. Yeah," Tina said, hardly looking at them. "You know what, S.J., there's something I want to give you . . . I knew I wanted to give it to you a long time ago, but I waited until now. Because I knew this time was coming and I just decided to save it."

I felt funny. "Listen, you don't have to give me anything," I said. "I'm not about to forget you."

Tina laughed loudly. "That's what Frances said!"

"You won't have any more Franceses," I said. "If anything goes wrong with your mother and living there and all, the Harrises would take you back in a minute. I bet even Ma and Pa would, you know? I bet they would."

Tina shook her head. "Nothing'll go wrong. I'll be okay now . . . I'm older, you know."

I nodded, not sure of what she meant.

"Anyway, I have this thing I wanna give you . . ." she looked down at her wrist and grinned. "I'd like to give you my watch, it's the most expensive thing I own, but . . . I stole it last fall from a drug store, and I just don't think . . ." she giggled, ". . . it would be right. To give you a hot watch."

"You mean it wasn't a present?" I asked, with make-believe surprise.

"No," she said, "but this was." She put her hand into her back pocket and pulled out the chain with the heart-locket on the end. "Here," she said. "Take it."

I had to remember I hadn't seen it before. "That's . . . beautiful," I said. "But there's no way I could take—"

"No, take it. Please." She pushed it at me.

I took it in both my hands and got my first close-up look at it. It *was* beautiful. The heart had a little design carved in it that had all turned black. "Bet it's very old," I said.

"Yeah, it's old. My mother got it from her mother who brought it over from Europe when they lived there, I don't know how long ago that was." Tina kept looking at it in my hand.

"Well, I can't take it. It's very special in your family. It belongs with you." I held it out to her.

"Open it," she said.

I didn't know it opened, but sure enough, there was the tiniest catch at the side of the heart. Inside was a picture of two faces, close together. One was a young-looking girl with long soft dark hair and the other was a little girl, grinning. They both looked happy.

"See?" Tina said. "That's my mother and me. It was a long time ago, I was little, but I remember that day. We took that picture at the penny arcade on

Broadway. They had this booth, where you put in some change and you get your picture taken. We had such a good time that day . . ."

Tina and her mother in the locket, I thought. That's how Tina's mother should look. The voices . . . the other voice . . . That's how Tina's mother should sound. Maybe that's who the other voice was supposed to be.

". . . so you take the locket now," Tina was saying. "Because I'm going there to be with her. And I don't need it any more.

I lifted it up and put the chain around my neck. "I would really like to have it," I said.

And it was time to go.

Mr. Harris had the back seat of his car packed with Tina's stuff and all of us were there to say good-bye, even Pa. Earl was working breakfast.

Katie went up to Tina and shook her hand. She was very serious and so was Tina. It made me smile a little. And Ma said we'd be glad to see her whenever she came and maybe she could stay with us a while in the winter. Pa said she was ten times more help than Earl and Tina smiled at that because he didn't really mean "ten times."

The car wasn't even out of sight when the crowd around Tina's cabin broke up. The twins and Bo headed for our house. Ma put her arm around Mrs. Harris and invited her over for coffee, and Pa went to the restaurant with Katie. Only I was left standing there . . .

"Oh, Sara?" Ma called over her shoulder.

"Yes?"

"Would you run down to Martha's and Jessie's and ask if we can expect any surprises over Labor Day? I want to know how full they'll be."

"Sure . . ." I turned and headed toward the Meridian. Labor Day . . . the last weekend of the summer, coming up already . . .

"Hi, Sarajane!"

I jumped. It was Betty Harmon. She was carrying a big pile of folded sheets and towels.

"Would you believe our washing machine broke down? I had to do this stuff over at Jessie's. Boy, I hope they get it fixed before Labor Day . . ." She went on walking toward Land's End.

Suddenly I remembered—I hadn't done the laundry in three whole days; I began to run—I had to get the Labor Day lists for Mama and hurry on back!

Halfway through the woods I slowed down . . . a yellowish rock caught my attention and I kicked it as I walked. I felt the locket bounce against my chest, so I held it tight in my fist and kicked the rock harder. It rolled ahead of me and hit a tree. I went over to the tree to pick it up again and then couldn't remember which rock it was. I started to sort some stones apart and then thought, why am I crouching here looking for some dumb rock? The locket wasn't bouncing any more but still I held it . . . The rock was yellow . . . where was it?